GANACHE AND FONDANT AND MURDER

Book Five: The Fiona Fleming Cozy Mysteries

PATTI LARSEN

Cover design by Christina Gaudet
www.castlekeepcreations.com

Thanks, Kirstin!

ISBN-13: 978-1-988700-53-3

CHAPTER ONE

Not to be indelicate about it, but if Mom made me eat one more bite of cake I was going to throw up. And not gently or modestly or in a ladylike fashion. I'd honestly ingested enough dessert in the last hour to sink a submarine with no end in sight.

Don't get me wrong. I loved my mother's baking. Dreamed about it, in fact, and rarely, if ever, turned down a slice after dinner. My cousin Robert's comments about my expanding backside, if true—and I still argued against his jerkish assessment—could only be blamed on Mom's cake.

But a girl has her limits, and I had finally reached mine, groaning as I sat back with both hands pressing to my distended stomach, burping softly around the chocolate, vanilla, red velvet, buttercream and banana that swam on the surface of a variety of other flavors I'd rather not taste again in reverse.

Gross.

From the crazed look in Mom's eyes, she didn't care I was ready to burst out of the waistband of my yoga pants. I'd never seen her so focused, so intensely driven, as I had the last three weeks. Ever since Olivia Walker, our town mayor if only still in that position by the skin of her heavily whitened teeth, offered Mom an exclusive opportunity my amazing mother couldn't even consider turning down.

"Too sweet?" Mom's green eyes narrowed while she examined my expression. Did she take the wince I shared with her as a judgment of her baking? "Too salty?"

I shook my head. "Delicious, Mom." Okay, so it came out weak and shaking and as close to a groan as I'd ever heard. "Honest, they're all—ugh—amazing."

Mom tapped her fingertips on the counter, glaring at the plate next to her and the remains of the selection of cakes she'd been stuffing into my mouth. "Maybe if I combined the maple with the vanilla and a hint of cinnamon topped with cream cheese icing…" Just the description was almost enough to send me over the edge. She whipped her head back around to glare at me. "Try this."

I stood abruptly, shaking my head, backing away from her while my pug, Petunia, licked her lips and moaned in hopeful frustration. She, at least, wouldn't turn Mom down but I absolutely had to. Gastric explosion: imminent.

"Mom, they're all fantastic." I waved off the fork laden with gooey goodness she jabbed at me. "You're going to crush your competition under a crust of sugary perfection. Trust me."

Mom snarled almost savagely, dropping the cutlery to the table, looking distinctly disappointed. "Fine, quit on me. Where's Daisy?"

My best friend had already fled, abandoning me to my mother's baking insanity with a headshake and a wincing smile of apology. I'd never forgive her for leaving me here like this when my mother had clearly lost her mind.

"Mom." I grasped her by both shoulders and shook her just a little while Petunia drooled next to me, staring up at us like she could will the cake to fall on the floor. I'd finally gotten her on a more regular feeding schedule and, would wonders never cease, she'd lost two pounds in the last two months. No way was she putting that weight back on.

"Fee." Mom tried to shrug me off, staring at her offerings again, biting her lower lip. "I really should add more red coloring to the velvet. It's a bit off-tone."

"It's perfect." I sat again, sighing. "Everything you make is perfect." She tsked at me but didn't argue as I held her hand. "You're going to shock and amaze the judges tomorrow, I know it."

And that, of course, was the crux of Lucy Fleming's loss of sanity and drive to stuff me until I burst. Olivia's offer, the big reveal of her January incentive to attract tourists, was right up my mother's alley.

"You really think so?" I wished Mom didn't doubt herself like that. Though I had to admit, the pressure had to be intense. "This is *Cake Or Break* we're talking about, Fee. National television."

She didn't have to tell me it was her favorite show. I already knew that, had been informed in no uncertain terms over and over and over again the last three weeks since Olivia dumped this special edition show being filmed here in town in Mom's lap and waltzed off. Leaving my mother to obsess over each and every recipe she'd ever made and turn Dad, Daisy and me into revolving sugar-crash test dummies.

"You got this, Mom," I said, carefully pushing the plate out of her reach, feeling my stomach sigh in relief. "They're going to love you."

"But I'm up against Janet Taylor." Last year's champion. I knew this already. Held onto my patience with the tips of my fingers. "And Molly Abbott." This year's top player and expected winner when the show wrapped up in April. "And Ron Williams, Fee. He's coming here, to judge me." Sigh. I didn't see the big deal in the pompous windbag, but then again, I'd only watched the show under duress when she forced me to, not out of enjoyment. While she sighed over his critical nastiness when he tore apart contestant's food offerings, I'd done my best not to eye-roll in her vicinity, wondering why anyone would put themselves in the position to be torn to bite-sized morsels of quivering, shattered confidence in the first place.

Part of me wanted to talk her out of it. Not that I didn't believe in her baking. Honestly? I spent ten years in New York City, and I'd never tasted food as good as my mother made. But I didn't trust my palate—or the judges, to be honest. While I knew Mom's skills were the bomb and my guests at Petunia's agreed, who knew what a big-time TV food judge would say about her baking? She was a grown woman, of course, she was. And yet, I couldn't help but feel protective of her. Mom didn't need some jackass of a jerk judge who liked being mean to people to eviscerate her on television because it improved his ratings.

Mom sat back, face falling. "Maybe I should just tell Olivia I can't do it."

Okay, so neither could I let her quit. "You are going to show them that Lucy Fleming knows her way around the kitchen." That got a small smile, a couple of blinks of her big, green eyes. "Mom, you already know you're awesome. If you want to go and have fun, I'm totally behind you. But do it because you want to, not because you need to prove something to the world." I leaned in and kissed her cheek. "A world that doesn't get to tell you you're not the most incredible mom, teacher, principal, baker and person ever. That's *your* job."

She was blinking again, eyes welling with tears before she lunged forward and hugged me. "I love you, Fee," she whispered, choked up.

Was going around. "I love you too, Mom." She shook a little then released me, giggling.

"I'm being silly." She patted her apron with both hands, looked up again, beamed a smile. "You're right. It's going to be fun. And I'm going to wipe the floor with them." She hesitated for the barest flash, and I finally understood what was behind her reticence, her nerves. Not the show at all, was it?

"How's the design for the wedding coming along?" I asked the question lightly, but I knew as soon as she flinched, I'd hit the nail on the nose. I'd been busy, so freaking busy, I hadn't had much time to ask her about Aundrea Wilkins and Pamela Shard's pending nuptials or my mother's part in it. Not while I juggled a house full of guests up until about a week ago and a giant renovation next door as the annex I bought last fall took shape. I tried to stay focused on Mom after I asked and not let my gaze go out the window of the kitchen toward the still standing fence and the towering form next door right now waiting, quiet and gutted after a long four weeks of demo.

I still had to pinch myself from time to time the place was actually mine. Here I thought Mom lost her marbles. I was the nutso one to take on another full-scale operation when Petunia's had me run off my feet like this.

"I'm not happy with the tier placement." Mom fussed a bit with the hem of her apron. "Or the tone of the ivory buttercream. I'm experimenting with a new pearl additive. But the flavor is hammered down." She smiled at that. "I'll be ready." Mom's hands kept moving, a sure sign she was agitated. "I just feel so bad for them, Fee."

I knew what she meant, had heard from Jared when I visited the annex yesterday. Aundrea's son was overseeing the renovation. I was grateful to have him, and though the conversion of his great-great aunt's former residence was his idea I didn't use that to bully him into helping me out. If anything, he seemed delighted at the chance to tackle the project. He was busier than me with seemingly endless expansions going on around town. Nice of him to make my job a priority. Didn't mean he stopped having time to share news, though.

"Jared said the Patterson clan is giving Aundrea a lot of crap for the wedding." Hardly shocking. Her own father forced her into marriage with Jared's father, the deceased Pete Wilkins, to keep her from revealing her love for Pamela. I had hoped they'd leave the now happy couple alone, but despite being mostly invisible to the rest of us, hiding out in their big mansion at the base of the mountain, their influence remained.

Mom sighed, nodded. "I see the strain in both of them," she said. "Pamela is ready to drag Aundrea off and elope."

"Maybe that would be a good idea." At least then it would be over and the Pattersons could move on to something else.

"Aundrea wants to make certain all of Reading knows she and Pamela are committed to each other."

Mom's jaw set, short nod affirmation she agreed.

"Has Vivian been giving you a hard time?" The nasty owner of the local bakery chain could kiss my butt. I knew it was eating Vivian up Mom was the one catering the wedding, with my bestie Daisy's help as event planner. Not to mention the fact the whole shebang was happening next door at the annex. I hardly minded sticking it to Vivian French. She and I had never had love lost between us, more so these days since she'd chosen to target my mother for wanting to sell her specialty cakes—like Vivian had a monopoly on baked goods in Reading—added to the charming attempt she'd made to undercut me by applying to town council for a permit to build a boutique hotel.

I'd shut that down by agreeing to the annex, though I was positive Olivia would be pressured into letting Vivian go ahead at some point. At least if the tourism rates continued to grow as quickly as they had been since our mayor's campaign to increase Reading's visibility in the world began.

I could tolerate Vivian coming after me. But my mother? Hell no.

Mom patted my hand, relaxing at last. "I'm fine, honey," she said. "It'll take a lot more than the likes of the Queen of Wheat to bring me down." So cute Mom had adopted my nickname for Vivian. Guess I wasn't the only one who thought it was funny. "Now, one more bite of the chocolate buttercream?"

Groan.

I didn't have to eat that bite, though honestly, I

would have gladly eaten a whole cake if I could have avoided what happened next. Not that Daisy's appearance was a bad thing. It was the tidings she brought that made my stomach flutter from more than an overdose of sweets.

I think we both knew something was wrong when she dashed through the door, though the instant Daisy spotted Mom she froze like she'd expected to find me alone. Petunia whined softly in the quiet that fell, instinctually knowing Daisy bore bad news, while my friend hesitated long enough Mom sighed.

"Just spit it out, Day," she said. "What's wrong?"

Daisy met my eyes then sagged, deflating. "It's not good." She winced.

"I figured as much." Mom's crisp reply seemed to give Daisy courage.

"French's Handmade Bakery was just announced as a major sponsor of the show tomorrow." Her large, gray eyes went from Mom to me and back again.

Whoops. That gave me instant heartburn. Wait, no. That was Mom's cake. But I'd blame my nemesis just because I could. "Vivian." I didn't intend for her name to sound like a swear word, but if the description fit…

"Of course, she's wormed her way in," Mom said, sounding utterly unsurprised and not a bit shaken. "Good for her." Like she meant it. "Considering none of her bakers were asked to participate," that a girl, Mom, "I've been expecting something like this."

"There's more." Because there was always more. "One of the judges had to back out, a death in the family."

Mom clutched her heart, mouth gaping. "Not Ron?" She might have hoped otherwise, but mine were pinned on his lack of participation. At least the other regular judges on the show always seemed to have tact and a bit of compassion in comparison.

Mom got her wish with Daisy's next words. "Melinda Whither," she said. "It's so last minute they had to recruit someone local."

Oh, craptastic. Like I didn't know who that local person just happened to be. Mom's frown told me she got it, too, even as Daisy finished in a half-whisper of dismay.

"Vivian," she said.

CHAPTER TWO

The three of us, my impatient pug not included, stayed silent a long moment while Petunia hummed her dissatisfaction at being ignored. I wondered how long we'd have hung there, none of us knowing what to say and a mix of emotions weighing the air in the room if it hadn't been for Dad's arrival.

He swept through the swinging door like he owned the place, a big smile on his face but stopped and did a double-take before meeting my eyes. "Who do I have to hunt down and kill before hiding the body so no one finds it?"

I snorted a laugh, Daisy too, grateful for the break in the mood. Mom didn't react well, though, still frowning, shaking her head a little as if having a conversation in her mind she wasn't enjoying. When she looked up again and met my gaze, she forced a smile.

"It'll all work out," she said. She swept off her apron, folding it and setting it aside, wiping her hands down the front of her jeans as if to settle herself before smiling again, still fake. "I'll see you in the morning?"

She turned and swept past Daisy, past Dad and out into the hall on her way to the foyer. My father's eyebrows raised, his face falling while Daisy joined me at the counter, one finger sliding into the chocolate icing that she sampled as Dad spoke.

"Tell me," he said, "so I know what to say to her in the car on the way home."

Didn't take long to fill him in. He grunted, scowling now, while I exchanged a nervous look with Daisy.

"Dad," I said. "Should we try to talk her out of going tomorrow?" I hated to do that. Mom had been so looking forward to it. Or was that torturing herself with it? Hard to know the difference. I didn't trust Vivian as far as I could throw her. Wait, throwing her somewhere felt like a great thing to do right about now. How about across the border into the next state so she couldn't do her best to humiliate my mother in public? Okay, I didn't know that was her goal, but I was not putting anything past her at this point.

"I think we all went into this knowing the show is likely rigged in favor of the two official contestants." Dad shrugged then, hands digging deep into the back pockets of his jeans. "We can't protect her from that, Fee. These shows are set up ahead of time. It's TV, for goodness's sake."

"She knows that." I felt a bit better.

"I wish I could protect her." His voice was so quiet I almost missed what he said. "But I wouldn't want to try, Fee. She's going to do what she wants, like always. No one has the right to tell her otherwise."

I hugged him, let him go as Mom called out for him from the foyer. He saluted and left, looking sad but determined and I hoped he did his best to buoy her as much as he could between now and tomorrow.

Of course, he would. But would it be enough?

"I shouldn't be thinking the worst is inevitable." I didn't realize I said that out loud to the sound of the front door closing behind my parents. Daisy started then smiled.

"You're right," she said, far too sparkly to mean it. "Lucy's going to kick butt."

She was. Then why was I so worried about her?

Daisy left shortly after while I deposited the remains of the cakes Mom made into the fridge, knowing despite the fact I was too full to consider even a crumb at the moment I'd be craving a slice with lunch tomorrow. While I didn't have sleepover guests to share with this week, the expanded meal times and dining experience took us past a true bed and breakfast these days and gave me opportunities to share such treats Mom left behind. I was fine with that, and I know my guests were delighted to sample Mom's cooking.

I did a quick round to make sure everything was okay, as I usually did at night, falling into routine. The front door lock snicked into place as the big grandfather clock in the foyer struck 9PM. I had a quiet week ahead, not a soul in sight or on the books, the January respite a huge relief. Any unscheduled guests could ring if they arrived later, but I was happy to close up for the evening. I drifted back to the kitchen after a fast tour upstairs, grabbing my winter coat and heading out into the garden with Petunia for her last outside potty before bed.

The last two months had been amazing and gratifying, the house full almost constantly up until the last week or so when the Christmas rush ended, and the new year vacationers went home. With Betty still bouncing back from her knee surgery, she and her sister, Mary, had gone into semi-retirement, Mom taking over for the silent Jones and Daisy helping me with the day-to-day. When the annex was ready—still no name, I had to do something about that—I'd have to hire some staff. But, for now, the four of us, with Dad for added assistance, seemed to have the whole thing handled.

I loved it that way. Me and my family and my business. I shivered in the chill of the January evening. The odd depression of last summer and fall had faded since I'd come to terms with being alone, or at least feeling like I was that way. Since I bought the annex and Jared started the demolition, I'd thrown myself into the life I'd fallen head over heels for, a life I never expected but was loving now that

I'd embraced it fully.

Sure, I still felt a bit down about Crew. He hadn't said a word about our last conversation, nor about how disappointed he'd been in me intruding in his case when Sadie died. I knew from poking around he'd been under a lot of pressure from Olivia and the council to include me and Dad into the murder cases we'd helped him solve. While I'd suspected as much that day in his office, a few questions broached over coffee here at Petunia's for the occasional local official to come for Mom's cooking had given me the answers I'd been looking for.

It was likely he'd never ask me out now. And I found I was okay with that. Mind you, I hadn't yet explored the dating site idea. The first time I'd dipped my nervous toes in those shark-infested waters had led me to deleting my listings after three unsolicited pictures of private parts and a handful of request for the same of mine triggered my gag reflex.

Whatever. I wasn't going to let loneliness get to me. I drew in a breath of sharp, cold air, Petunia waddling toward the kitchen door, soft puffs of mist rising from her panting mouth as she led me back inside. My gaze settled on the dark bulk of the annex next door, and I smiled at its quiet potential.

No Crew? No problem. Didn't need him or anyone else. My life was coming together. Oh, and one more thing I'd decided since the fake psychic's murder was resolved in the arrest of Amos Cortez. If I was unlucky enough to stumble into another death by foul play? No one—not a single soul and certainly not Crew Turner—was going to stop me from being a busybody. I refused to apologize for my natural aptitude for curiosity ever again.

Mind you, not being part of a murder investigation because I either found the body or had the victim die in my lap? Yeah, that would be good, too.

As I turned back to the house, I couldn't help but think about Mom. And then Dad as I locked the door and shucked off my coat, hanging it by the exit. Petunia waited at the fridge for her night snack of fruit while I considered my dad. He'd been great to have around, so helpful and eager to do whatever I needed. I wondered if he felt lost, if retiring had been a bad choice. Then again, having him here had been a blessing, so I hoped he loved it as much as I did.

I just wished I could shake the anxiety I felt when I thought about the business card with the woman's name written on it in Malcolm Murray's handwriting. It still sat in my music box, with the scrap of map and the gold coin Grandmother Iris left me, waiting for me to hunt down Siobhan Doyle and find out what her connection was to Dad.

I'd meant to investigate, honest. And every time I'd decided it was the right moment, I distracted myself with other things. Did that mean I was a coward? Or that the past didn't matter to me as much as I thought it did?

Whatever the case, as I closed the fridge door and handed Petunia her half a banana and six strawberries in a small dish, I shrugged off the impulse to judge myself for not following my nose.

That was the best part about deciding no one got to tell me what to do. It worked both ways, right?

Right.

CHAPTER THREE

The house felt quiet, anticipating guests who were a week away. Funny, it felt almost like a living, breathing thing when it was full of visitors and a sleeping giant when no one filled the rooms upstairs. But I never felt uncomfortable here when I was alone. I guess that was as good a sign as I was getting I'd fallen in love with my life.

I went downstairs to my apartment, Petunia huffing her waddling way in front of me. Two pounds lost or not, she had a way to go yet, but I was hopeful I had her on track. I loved her fat little butt and wanted to keep her around as long as possible.

As I passed the bottom of the landing, I remembered the lock on my door wasn't working as well as I'd like, sticking on occasion. My mind turned over the possibility of having Jared's crew do some small jobs around this place, too, in prep for the busy spring season, a list growing in my head.

If Vivian was planning to open her own place next year, I'd have to be sure Petunia's and the annex were both in top shape. Though I did admit her plans for a boutique hotel sounded a lot like something I couldn't contend with, nor would want to. Hers would likely be the epitome of prissy princess, pink and ivory and sparkling like an uber-modern palace for those who could afford it. My setup was more on the nostalgic, quaint side. Impossible to compare, like shining treasure held up against whatever steaming pile of crap she came up with. Snort.

I wasn't fooling myself as I sank into the cushions of my sofa, Petunia hopping up next to me, groaning softly while she settled in, chin on my lap, bulging eyes locked on me until I rubbed her black ears. Whatever Vivian came up with would be gorgeous, I had zero doubt of that. I'd just have to deal with it when the time came and be grateful for the head start on my own reputation.

Besides, there was a good chance she was going to do her best to hurt my mother tomorrow and that would mean I'd be in the middle of another murder investigation with her as the victim. Likely the guilty party at last.

At least it would mean the end of Vivian French.

I flipped open my laptop to check my website, grinning at how great it looked. While Denver Hatch had done well for himself selling the design for his holographic invention to a game company, he'd chosen to stay here in Reading full-time. Might have had something to do with the fact he and his grandfather, Oliver Watters, were now thick as thieves. The old historian and antique dealer had vastly improved his attitude since he and Denver met. More likely, though, Denver's choice to stay was due to the fact Alice Moore moved into his grandmother's place with him. The sweet couple ran their own psychic investigation company from the house, which cracked me up, considering Sadie had been a hack and a fraud her whole life. Having those two take on the fake psychic's kind head-on was my sort of sweet revenge.

Whether he felt gratitude for me saving his butt at Halloween from the gun of Amos Cortez or he just liked me, Denver was kind enough to help me with my site and optimizing my social media—whatever that meant—that increased my visibility online.

I'm sure Alice would agree when I said he was a total keeper.

Trouble with focusing on the internet was my access to instantaneous reaction from my clients. While a good thing to know if they enjoyed their experiences or not in our town and my B&B, the positive reviews inflated my ego far too much while the nasty ones could knock me down just as fast. Honestly, I really needed to stop reading them.

Taking my own advice (yeah, right) I skimmed the current crop of comments posted the last three weeks, most of them delightful, though I scowled in irritation at the one that mentioned Petunia—the pug, not the house—and her flatulence. The woman's dislike for my dog's "disgusting farts" got my back up, as did her snide comment about the "revolting poop" problem in the garden.

Excuse me. I cleaned up after my pug. Oh, and said client wasn't ever coming back to my establishment until I did the right thing and did away with Petunia and her biological processes?

Then she'd be waiting a very long time while my darling girl and I carried on. Seriously. The woman could suck it.

I snorted at my reaction to the one-star and patted Petunia who opened her sleepy eyes in response to the touch. "What do you think of that review, missy?" She groaned and closed her eyes again, farting faintly. I laughed. "Yeah," I said. "Me too."

It was nerve-wracking, though, if I was going to be honest with myself. I hated that clench of my stomach when I got an email about a new review, the constant concern I'd bitten off more than I could chew and that I was missing things, not getting it right. And now there was the annex to worry about. I'd already started taking bookings based on the timeline Jared gave me and fretted occasionally about doing so. May was a long way off but not that long and the pending deadline loomed over me in a growing swell of anxiety. I couldn't just wait until the work was done to start filling the rooms that were lucky if they had plumbing yet. I had to pay for the place, after all, even if it meant pushing my comfort and trusting Jared.

While I'd gotten a great deal on the house next door thanks to his kindness, I still had a large chunk of money invested in it and a rapidly growing line of credit to cover.

Kind of fun, too, though. Especially looking at designs with Daisy and colors with Alicia. Both had impeccable taste, way better than mine. The annex was going to be stunning when it was done. Now I just needed a name already.

I headed to bed at last, Petunia creaking her way up the stairs to the bed, settling next to my pillow while I stared down at my music box and shook my head.

Daisy had taken the letters Daniel Munroe wrote to Grandmother Iris, looking for a good name for the annex. And, she admitted, for clues to the Reading hoard, neither of which I held out much hope for. Two big treasure hunters had been in town last fall, and both debunked the idea that the pirate founder of our home even had anything to hide. My grandmother's secret she passed to me was likely just a scavenger hunt to nothing. Otherwise, why wouldn't she have tracked the treasure down herself?

Bed never felt so good, though as I drifted to sleep, I thought again about Dad, about Malcolm and Siobhan Doyle.

Was it the overload of sugar in my stomach or the thoughts in my head that gave me nightmares?

CHAPTER FOUR

Dad's text woke me early. *Something came up. Pick up Mom? Meet you at the Lodge.*

Hrumph. He'd better not miss her debut as a baking superstar or neither of us would hear the end of it. The original chime was followed by a rapid-fire slew of musical pings as my phone delivered texts from my mother that told me, in no uncertain terms, I was in for a very, very bad morning.

8AM sharp
Wear something nice
Don't be late
Bring my red spatula
Never mind found it
Where's my diamond earrings?
That was for your father

8AM SHARP

And that was just a selection of the madness. Sigh.

Mom was waiting for me at the door when I pulled up to her front walk. I didn't get to exit the car to help her down the path, even though there was no need. Dad did a great job clearing snow and ice from the stone. Still, I was positive if Mom wasn't careful, she'd fall anyway she was moving so fast.

She skidded into the street in her boots, throwing herself into the front seat and slamming the door, face intent and cheeks pink. "Let's go, I don't want to be late."

Um, it was 8AM and she wasn't supposed to be there until 9:30. "Mom, we have lots of—"

"Fiona." She snapped my name the instant her seatbelt buckle clicked home. "Drive!"

Okay then, crazy lady.

I yawned into the chill air, the heater of my car catching up slowly as we cruised through town. The faint snowfall of the two nights ago still clung to people's lawns, making everything crisp and white, the cold temperatures not allowing for it to turn to the brown slushiness I hated about winter. The mountains towered over us, more white punctuated by evergreens, paths cut into the forest where the White Valley Ski Lodge dominated. Our destination beckoned, my car chugging up the highway toward the main lodge while Mom squirmed and fretted.

I normally rose at 6AM so her seven o'clock call hadn't been all that intrusive. Still, I'd been forced to abandon Betty and Mary to the local breakfast crowd to hustle to Mom's early, thinking I had way more time than she planned.

"Excited?" I tried to crack the chill of our trip—the heater had kicked in but Mom's temperature hadn't shifted—with a question, but my mother just grunted at me and stayed quiet. From the small circles of red at the tips of her cheekbones and the paleness of the rest of her, she was working herself into a frenzy of nerves that could lead her to disaster.

This was going to stop right now, or I was turning this car around and taking her home and she could find her own ride to the Lodge. Before she could stop me, squeaking her upset at my grim determination, I pulled over to the side of the road, waving off a truck that laid on the horn and turned to face her. Mom met my eyes with her own wide in shock and frustration, spluttering at me.

"Keep going! I'm going to be—"

I shut her down with a hug. "Mom," I said. "Breathe."

She tried to brush me off, but I wasn't having any.

"Fiona Fleming," she said.

"Lucy Fleming," I answered.

She giggled a bit, uncoiled just enough I felt it was safe to let her go.

"Oh, Fee," she said in a tiny voice, "I'm so scared."

That had to have been one of the hardest things she'd ever said. I'd seen my mother face down a lot of things in her life with determination and courage and the kind of cheerfully firm optimism that I aspired to. For her to admit to me she was afraid? Epic.

"Of what?" I didn't tease her, asked her point-blank. "Tell me specifically." Did she recognize her own beginnings of a pep talk in my command?

She swallowed, touched her hair with one gloved hand. "Failing?"

"The only way you can fail is if you quit." That was her line, verbatim. She'd said it to me so many times as a kid I knew it by rote. Just like what came after. "Next?"

Mom finally recognized what I was doing, who I was being for her because she smiled. "Being judged."

"Are you going to do your best?" I waited while she nodded eagerly. "Are you going to cheat or lie or do something you can't be proud of?" She shook her head this time, eyes laughing, lips twitching. Much better and a delight to turn Lucy Fleming loose on Lucy Fleming. I really was morphing into my own mother, wasn't I? "Are you ready for this?" Another nod. "Then the only judging you have to worry about is your own. Because as long as you do your best no one gets a say. Anything else?"

Mom embraced me. "When did you get so smart?"

"I learned from the best." I kissed her and grinned. "Ready?"

She squeezed my hand, beamed a real smile.

"Ready, Mom."

Giggle. Awesome.

The rest of the drive we cranked some music on the radio and sang at the top of our lungs. I hadn't done that with my mother for years, not since we used to drive to the coast with Dad behind the wheel, me and Mom and sometimes Daisy belting out our favorite songs while my father grinned and tried to join us though he sounded like a bullfrog with a serious case of tonsillitis.

By the time we reached the front entrance of the Lodge, Mom was relaxed, composed and herself. I followed her inside, so grateful I had the chance to help and that proud of her for being amazing I could have exploded.

Instead, I followed her through the lobby, waving at Alicia behind the front desk who waved eagerly back, gesturing for me to wait. Mom moved on ahead of me, following the signs for the taping into the dining room while I watched her go, Alicia hurrying to my side. She hugged me quickly, cheeks flushed, eyes bright.

"Your mother is going to clean up," she said. I grinned back, hoping she was right, that Dad's pessimism wasn't more accurate. I frowned a little that he wasn't here yet, though I was happy I had the chance to diffuse Mom before she baked.

"Everything ready to go?" I glanced at the entry to the dining room across the lobby, guests drifting past in their puffy coats and ski pants, the Lodge clearly packed for the week even if I was getting a break. This resort had suffered no end of issues since opening, but it seemed like I was receiving fewer calls to take on guests due to problems cropping up, so hopefully Jared had reversed the bulk of his cheating father's fraudulent construction practices and that the Lodge was now fully operational.

"All set," Alicia said, eyes sparkling. "It's so exciting. Oh, and don't forget to pop over to the annex and check out the flooring, would you?" Right, I had to get on that. "I know you said to just pick one, but I want to be sure you love it before it's installed. And I left you some cutlery samples, too. Have you decided about the spa in the basement yet?" Did she have any idea she was making my head hurt? Doubtful. Nervousness woke in my stomach for me instead of Mom as I thought about just how much there was to do and the giant leap I'd taken. "We need to order some equipment if you think you want to go ahead."

Mind spinning, I managed a grin despite myself. Not caving and crumbling under pressure. This was fun, right? Absolutely. "I promise I'll get right on it. But Mom." I gestured at the dining room doors.

Alicia laughed. "I'm sorry, of course. Go! I'll talk with you later. Wish her luck for me." She bustled off in her dark suit and heels, another confident and powerful woman in my life. I'd take as many as I could get.

When I turned to head for the set, I spotted Malcolm Murry heading toward me and froze in place, shocked to find him here. Especially as he was exiting the dining room. What business did he have with the TV show? The guy was practically the head of Reading's Irish mob. Okay, not practically. He was the mob. Who was he here to see?

Malcolm approached, gray hair sparkling in contrast to the deep black wool of his peacoat, though his usual smile was missing. He'd stopped coming to Petunia's for tea shortly after he handed me the woman's name on the card in the back of his black car. As if doing so divested him of the need to show me kindness. Instead, he glared at me like I was some kind of obstacle in his way before he spoke, Irish accent harsh.

"Fiona," he said. "Looked up that name yet, have you?"

He didn't have to be so blatant about it. "I haven't had a chance," I said, knowing it sounded weak and pathetic. He scowled darker while I glanced at the doors to the set. "What are you doing here?" He wasn't the only one with a corner market on blunt.

"My business," he snapped, "not yours." He strode off then, leaving me to gape after him, his two dark-suited and long-coated bully boys trailing behind him, though one turned and met my eyes, his expression almost… what? Sad?

Weird. What was he upset about?

I let it go, knowing I'd somehow let Malcolm down but refusing to feel bad about it. I'd get to it in my time. When I wanted answers. Right now, I was here for my mother.

CHAPTER FIVE

I passed through the doors to the dining room while a young woman with a clipboard argued with an older gentleman in a bright yellow ski suit about breakfast being relocated to another part of the lodge, knowing it was very likely I wasn't supposed to be sneaking past her without checking in. Whoopsie, my bad. On the other side of the heavy curtain and crappy rear of a wall of plywood I was transported from the back side of what looked like a huge mess and into the polished and familiar set of *Cake Or Break*.

Amazement froze me for a moment when I looked around, brilliant lights hanging overhead, three big cameras hunched like bulky robots waiting for commands in the corners, a variety of crew hustling around with headphones and walkie talkies while I did my best to pull myself together in the bright white and yellowness of the décor and act like I was supposed to be there.

The trio of kitchens set up parallel to each other stood on my right side, stainless steel counters and appliances flanking shelving stuffed with every imaginable baking item known to humanity, and likely a lot that weren't. The show was known to push bakers to use unusual ingredients at times, and I wondered how Mom would handle a tin of anchovies like I'd seen tossed at one baker in the last episode I'd seen.

On my left, the judge's table stood at least a foot higher than floor level with matching white leather stools waiting for the official butts to warm them. I'd never been on a live set before, so I kept my head down and set my sights on Mom who stood next to a young woman in a pretty pink dress, her light brown hair curled around her face.

I almost stumbled at the sight of Vivian French as she entered at the side of another woman—one I recognized as Janet Taylor, last year's winner—the two with their heads together, whispering. I didn't like the look of their closeness, or how Janet seemed to command the stage, showing Vivian through her kitchen like it was her kingdom.

Whatever. Vivian looked up, caught me watching and scowled while I scowled right back before jabbing my finger at my mother, then at her. The message had to be clear. Screw with Mom, play her false? She'd pay.

Vivian tossed her head and turned her back on me, leaving me to fume as I stalked the rest of the way to Mom's side without lunging for the arrogant Queen of Wheat while my mind unwound ways to make her suffer. Mom was too wrapped up in her own chat with a slim young woman with honey-brown hair to notice my mood. I quickly wiped the frustrated snarl off my face—look at me, putting Mom first—and managed to smile when she spun on me and beamed.

"Fee!" Her fingernails dug into my arm even through my winter coat as she tugged me close to her hip, almost shoving me forward at the smiling woman. I recognized her, too, from the shows Mom made me watch the last three weeks. Molly Abbot shook my hand, her fingers cold to the touch, angular cheekbones and overlarge hazel eyes making her seem ethereal. I often wondered how someone who made a living from sugar and wheat could ever be so tiny, hating the jab of jealousy as I thought about my own backside and the cake Mom had been forcing down my throat.

Yeah. I was so done with dessert from now on.

"A pleasure to meet you, Miss Fleming," Molly said. "Your mother tells me you have a lovely bed and breakfast in town?"

My mother nodded, answering for me, her excitement obvious in the rapid-fire chatter she couldn't seem to hold back. "I love working in her kitchen," she gushed. "And the new annex will have an even bigger space. I can't wait to start baking there." Really? She hadn't said as much to me. Nice to know she was so excited, though. "Fee, this is Molly Abbott, this season's star."

She'd clearly forgotten she'd forced me to sit in front of the television for a binge session of the last and this season, so I'd know everyone by face and name. Molly flushed slightly, shrugging a bit as if Mom's label made her uncomfortable.

"I haven't won yet," she said, thin lips quivering. "It certainly would be nice, though, wouldn't it?" What made her so nervous all of a sudden? The way she rubbed one thin arm with her free hand across the front of her body like she was subconsciously protecting herself from something? Or how she glanced around, ducking her head when she did? If she just harbored a nervous personality, she'd chosen the wrong vehicle for her success. Being on a reality show wasn't exactly for shrinking violets.

Mom didn't seem to notice, those nails digging into me again. She needed to clip them or something. "Everyone knows you're going to win, dear," she gushed. "I'm just so delighted to get to meet you before you do!"

Molly laughed, a quivering sound. "You're too kind, Lucy. I can't wait to see what you come up with."

Mom swatted the air between them. "This is just a silly special," she said. "I have no illusions." Oh, really? Since when, Lucy Fleming? "But I do have a trick or two up my sleeve."

Molly seemed to relax as the conversation turned to baking, hand falling from the death grasp on her upper arm while she leaned into Mom. "Just please, don't let them give us anything fishy for the challenge!" She rolled her eyes while Mom groaned. "I almost died when I had to use oysters in my cheesecake three episodes ago."

Ew. I forgot about that. But the judges loved her savory concoction and gave her top marks.

"Are you always nervous or is it just me?" Mom fanned her face with her free hand, and I was a bit shocked she chose to be candid with Molly. But the young baker's kindness radiated from her as she grasped for Mom's wrist and gently held it, smile back in place, hazel eyes locked on my mother.

"Every time," she said. "Every single time, Lucy. First show? I had to keep a bucket backstage just in case." She tossed her long hair as she laughed. "You're going to be great. Just focus on baking. That's all that matters."

Mom gulped but seemed comforted by Molly's support and I nodded pointedly at her when my mother turned with a beaming smile and looked over the three kitchens. Molly's answering, knowing grin told me she was about as good a person as I could hope for.

The crew had settled into their positions while we talked, a handsome young man in a headset and carrying a tablet smiling his approach to us. I instantly flinched, knowing he was about to kick me out when he instead spoke to Molly.

"We're about ten minutes out," he said in his smooth tenor. An actor, perhaps, working behind the scenes? I heard it was common. Molly flushed slightly, looking away while he did the same. Adorable, these two. Did either of them know the other was totally infatuated or were they both trying to hide it? Surely this kind of innocence couldn't survive reality television.

I could dream, though.

He then turned to Mom with a smile just as sweet, if without the underscore of longing. "Lucy, are you ready?"

She tittered. Seriously tittered, the tiniest little vibration of a sound that made me stare with my mouth open such a mouse-like squeak could come from my mother.

"As ready as I'm getting, Dale," she said, hand on his forearm like he was an old friend. "Let's bake!"

He met my eyes, his a lovely sea green, square jaw clean-shaven, blond hair short enough to be professional but just long enough to be stylish. His dark blue golf shirt, the show's logo over his heart, pulled tight across his broad chest and while he wasn't overly tall, he'd do. Not to steal a metaphor while standing on a baking show stage, but I wouldn't kick him out of bed for eating cupcakes.

"Dale Lewis, my daughter, Fiona." Mom hadn't lost her gushiness or her manners, apparently. "Dale's our production assistant." She giggled like that was funny for some reason. I shook Dale's hand while he reciprocated, pausing a moment with his eyes far away before dropping my fingers from his.

"Roger that." His smile and attention returned. "Ladies, if you'd please make your way to the green room?"

Mom clapped in visible excitement, turning to blow me a kiss before hurrying off with Molly. It was nice to see the taller, slim form of the young woman leaning over Mom, paying her close attention. At least she seemed lovely enough. Some of my concern for Mom's wellbeing faded as they disappeared around the corner of the set and out of sight. It sounded like my mother wasn't gunning for top spot and would be perfectly fine losing to her new bestie.

At least, I hoped that was the case. As long as she wasn't fooling herself. I was here, just in case of a meltdown, though again I frowned at my watch and looked over my shoulder. Where was Dad?

"Your mother is a doll," Dale said, winking with a grin.

"My mother," I groaned, "has lost her mind." I hesitated before asking my next question in a hushed tone of voice. "Is the show fair, Dale?"

He flinched, smile fading, mouth open to answer when we were interrupted. The short, stocky woman in thick black glasses, her hair dyed an amazing color of pink, scowled up at me before jerking her thumb at the door.

"No visitors on set." She stalked away without another word, black t-shirt and pants both with a dusting of what looked like flour across her waist.

Crap. I really wanted to watch. Shouldn't have

been worried, though. Dale rolled his eyes at me, winked again and led me with a gentle hand on my elbow to a far corner of the set, just off the white flooring and tucked behind a large shelving unit.

"Clara Clark," he said. "She's the show creator." I nodded. "And showrunner, big boss lady. She's usually nice, but stress can make her a bit of a you-know-what." He sat me on an extra stool and grinned. "Someone put a giant-sized bee in her bonnet over this special, let me tell you." His eye roll was legendary, low whistle to match.

I grinned. "Pretty sure the offending insect is our town mayor." Speak of the queen buzz, she swept onto the set from backstage, embracing Clara like they were old friends. I wasn't watching her, though, could care less about Olivia's political routine. Instead, I watched the tall, handsome older gentleman in the three-piece suit and bow tie who strode onto set like he ruled from a sugar throne, towering over everyone, his booming laugh unmistakable.

Dale didn't seem impressed, about as much as the tall, slender woman standing next to the laughing judge, glaring up at him. "I take it you recognize Ron Williams?" I nodded. "And his wife, Bonnie." I hadn't seen her before, assumed she wasn't part of the show. It was apparent as she turned away from him and joined Olivia and Clara that was the case. Ron, on the other hand, his thick head of silver hair swept back into a stunning coif, air of charisma reaching me across the set, seemed in his element, shaking Olivia's hand, waving at the crew who unenthusiastically waved back.

Interesting dynamics. Dale turned back toward me, hand going to the mouthpiece of his headset.

"On my way." He backed up a step, waving a little. "Just stay out of sight and no one will bother you, okay?"

I huddled there, thankful partly but actually wishing I could be anywhere but there, hiding in a corner behind equipment while my mother was alone and vulnerable. I had to shake that off. Dale hadn't answered my question about the show's fairness, but this was a special. Surely the normal shenanigans of the season wouldn't be in evidence. Mom would bake, they'd eat it and like it or not like it and we'd all go home.

I spotted Dale at the door, scowling, a familiar-looking middle-aged woman trying to push past him. Wait, I knew her from the show, didn't I? Wasn't she on last season? The episodes all ran together, and I honestly hadn't been paying as close attention as I should have. She looked upset, regardless, near tears, and though he was gentle enough with her he finally succeeded in banishing her from the set. I didn't get to ponder what she was doing here or what her problem was, because a moment later, to my shock and acute discomfort, I was no longer alone.

With his handsome face in a tight mask of unhappiness, Sheriff Crew Turner nodded down at me like he would rather be anywhere else but next to me.

CHAPTER SIX

I was about to take it personally, deeply hurt in that instant of his crankiness, just as he cast his blue-eyed gaze over the set with a twist to his wide mouth.

"Hollywood," he grumbled. "I thought I left this crap behind in California."

I swallowed my moment of agony with the kind of surprised zing that made me blush. Okay, and maybe it was the scent of him hovering there, coffee and chocolatey caramelish deliciousness that reminded me my last relationship was about a year and a half ago. A relationship that ended badly with me swearing off men forever and ever that lasted until I saw Crew for the first time when I returned home to Reading and found he'd taken Dad's place as sheriff. Not to mention the fabric softener he used on his clothes mingling with the natural scent of him that invaded my personal space and made me tingle in very private places.

Why oh, why was he just so yumtastic without a chance in hell I'd get to sample his wares? It had been two months since we talked, since the ill-fated murder of Sadie Hatch and Crew's no-nonsense disappointment he expressed in a way that convinced me any chance I ever had to find out if we could be an item died with her and my need to poke my nose in where it wasn't wanted. I'd given up on me and Crew and decided to explore other, less stressful, opportunities.

That's why I wasn't expecting his slightly nervous smile, the sweet way he seemed to soften as he ran one big hand through his dark hair when he relaxed next to me, the soft sigh of his sheriff's jacket loud in the quiet between us. His black waves always seemed in need of a trim, the shining silkiness of it hanging over his collar, the faintest stubble darkening his broad jaw. There was nothing arrogant or angry about him when his blue eyes met mine again, soft around the corners. Considering he usually had a tic under his left one and a vein standing out on his forehead when he addressed me, it was a nice change to see him smile.

Now, the question was, could I keep it together and not screw up this seeming change of demeanor and attitude when it came to me? I wasn't holding my breath. No, wait, I was, but for different reasons tied to my silly heart going pitter-pat.

"Here for Lucy?" He kept his voice pitched low, almost intimate. I shivered just a little, smacking myself internally for my reaction. We were trapped in a limited space, and he was forced to make it work, not whispering sweet nothings. I really needed to start dating so I could let go of this ridiculous obsession I seemed to have with wanting him to like me. It was obvious, really, nothing had changed, and he'd chosen to be nice and make small talk because the alternative was an uncomfortable silence.

Yeah, I really went all the way from one end of the spectrum to another in less than two seconds.

"Yes, for Mom. She's baking." Oh my god, what was wrong with me? "I'm worried about her." Okay, yes, I was blurty, had a blurtiness problem my whole life, so nothing new there. Guilty. But holy cow, Fee. Did I have to blurt all over Crew like this? "You're doing security?"

Crew didn't seem to take anything that tumbled out of my mouth the wrong way, didn't snort or roll his eyes or act disdainful, bless his heart. Instead, he bobbed a nod, leaning closer, whispering as Dale's voice called out on the set, prepping for filming.

"Olivia wanted me here." He sounded like he thought it was a waste of time. "I disagreed."

"And she won?" I winced, wondering if he'd think I was being facetious. Instead, blue eyes sparkling, he flashed his white teeth in a half-smile, half-snarl. I wondered if he knew just how freaking sexy he looked in that moment.

Fiona Fleming. Stop it right now.

"Like always," he said, oblivious to my internal battle with hormones and longing and the need to pull up my big girl panties and shed this attraction I had for him. "Pretty typical of the strong women in this town, though."

That was oddly… complimentary, maybe? About Olivia? No, Mom, right? Um, wait, why was he looking at me like that. Was he talking about *me*? A spark of maybe, just maybe, flickered into life in my heart.

"Should put it on our travel brochures," I said. And I'd just taken awkward to a double face-palm level previously unachieved by a redhead in serious need of a date.

Crew chuckled instead of my expectation he'd not get the joke. "A little warning ahead of time would have been nice," he said. "Before I took the job."

"Sorry about that," I said. "I wasn't here to write the blurb. I'll make sure the next handsome sheriff who moves to town has tons of advanced notice. You know, so he can run screaming before it's too late."

Blue eyes sparked, full lips lifted in a smile. I was having a conversation with Crew, and it wasn't sucking and I wasn't making a fool of myself. He got my jokes, he got me. Was this what heaven was supposed to feel like? Yes. Yes, I think so.

"I wouldn't bother," he said, deep voice a bit rough before he cleared his throat. "I'm not going anywhere." He hesitated before leaning closer, smile fading. "I was hoping I could talk to you later. About something." He cleared his throat again. Was he getting a cold? "Private?"

Gulp. "Sure. You can come by Petunia's?" How could I sound so relaxed and calm when my little heart leaped so hard and high, I was sure it would burst from me and land at his feet. Private? Did that mean he was finally going to ask me out? No way, it couldn't be. The conversation we'd had in my backyard last April was so far gone it was like it never happened. And yet when his smile came back, kind and a little nervous, I leaped to the conclusion without proof and didn't care to argue about it.

"Great," he said. "I'll pop by. Maybe tomorrow night?" Was that hope in his voice?

Squeal. My phone hummed, caught my hissing attention and I silenced it in anticipation of being yelled at for the faint sound without answering Crew's question. When I checked the screen, it was a text from Dad, that he was held up. I frowned at the message while I tucked it in my pocket, wondering what could be keeping him from Mom's big day.

If he was late, I'd kill him. Made me think about Malcolm, though, and before I could consider what I was about to do, I firmly squashed the rapport I'd been building with the handsome man beside me by asking an inappropriate question instead of answering his more enticing one.

"What do you know about my dad and Malcolm Murray?"

I might as well have told him I found another

dead body. Crew's gaze flattened out, but he didn't overreact. Instead, he looked away, face composed, our lovely, connected moment over. "I think they're getting started," he said. Which was about all I was going to get from him, I guess.

Fiona Fleming, could you be more of an idiot?

I sat there in my private misery, wishing I could take my question back, as the real drama of the day unfolded before me.

CHAPTER SEVEN

I don't know what I was expecting. A lot more excitement, that's for certain. Instead, I caught myself yawning more and more frequently in the next several hours as the tedium of filming unfolded before me. The process had zero resemblance to the final product, the introductions of the judges and the contestants done in a multitude of takes that seemed to wind out into infinity before any baking actually happened.

If I had to sit there much longer I'd be asleep.

Crew didn't seem to be faring much better, blue eyes glazing over, the occasional sigh of unhappy boredom making me yawn harder. Still, it was at least initially interesting to see how a show was made, if only for my own curiosity's satisfaction. And to distract us both from the fact I'd nipped whatever shining thing had been sparking between us when I doused its young flame with stupidity.

Focus on the show and not your self-inflicted single womanhood, Fee.

I was already familiar with the cast, at least, so there weren't any surprises there, when a young woman in a headset like Dale's stepped out, tablet in hand.

"Quiet on set!"

The judges were already seated, Olivia between Ron and the testy-looking Vivian, though when the camera rolled the bakery maven's face settled into a more pleasing, if fake, expression of marginal happiness. Like Vivian knew what the word even meant. I chose to ignore her while the host, Patrice York, introduced her, Olivia and then, with gushing enthusiasm, Ron Williams, to the camera.

"We're so delighted to present this special edition of *Cake or Break* in the lovely town of Reading, Vermont," she said, perky tone making my teeth ache. She smiled her chicklet white grin into the hulking camera, portly operator standing behind it with an expression about as bored as mine. "But being on location doesn't mean we take things easy on our contestants, does it, judges?"

Murmurs of agreement followed Clara's sharp, "Cut!" To which Patrice tsked her irritation, her beaming smile vanished to a nasty scowl.

"What was wrong with that?" Her annoyance showed on the crew's faces, too, and I wondered about Clara's management style. Or maybe this was just the business? "We agreed on that script, Clara."

"You're leaning into it too much," the showrunner snapped. "Stop trying to act and just deliver the lines, Patrice."

The young woman with the tablet called them to order with a sharp, "Frame!" and Patrice's face instantly transformed from petulant pissed off into her perky delight all over again.

Crew snorted next to me while I shook my head. "Ridiculous," he whispered.

"Tell me about it." I was just grateful for the chance to change the subject and maybe not make him mad all over again.

"I should have sent Jill. This is a waste of time." His jaw jumped a bit while Dale's head whipped around, halfway across the room, and he raised one finger to his lips in the universal sign we should shut up already.

Whoops. That gesture did nothing for Crew's mood and when he fell silent again it was with a steady, burning glare right at Olivia.

Well, at least he was blaming someone else for his unhappiness for a change. I glanced down as he leaned around me to rest one hand on the rack, his sleeve pulling up to expose the off-center compass tattooed on the inside of his wrist. The sight of it made me shiver just a little, a reminder I'd failed to pursue the hints and leads my grandmother left me about the Reading treasure hoard. I was fairly certain it was all bunk, and any kind of open investigation would just make everyone think I was more of a crackpot than they already did, not to mention the solid debunking of the myth of the gold and jewels being hidden somewhere in town. Still, I loved a good mystery and the prodding reminders made goosebumps rise. Enough I grinned to myself like a little kid with a secret.

Wouldn't hurt to do a bit of digging, right? Starting with why Crew Turner, a guy from the other side of the country, had a tattoo that seemed to resemble the compass on the map piece I owned? Then again, it was a fairly familiar symbol, and the coincidence was likely nothing more than that. And yet, I had never discovered what led Crew here in the first place, so far from California. Yes, he moved here after the loss of his beloved wife to cancer. But why Reading? Another coincidence?

Questions for later. If and when—heavy on the if—he actually came to see me after all. Crap, I'd forgotten to confirm that tomorrow night was okay, and it was totally too late for that without looking like an idiot. I squirmed over how to handle reopening the topic without arriving at a suitable solution. Too late anyway. With the introductions and the preliminary bits filmed, the crew moved on to the good part—the baking.

This time, at least, the filming went straight through, though it was hard to see past the multiple cameras, as operators in a strange-looking harness with bulky equipment strapped to them hurried about, one for each kitchen, catching different angles as the larger cameras slid across the floor on silent wheels. A long, thick pole bobbed slowly down into the center of the set, another camera mounted on the end, swinging with a ballet performance-like precision, avoiding taking out the crowd on the ground in a smooth dance that wowed more than the baking. It was fascinating to watch the interweaving of the three perspectives and I realized only then just how complicated the whole show actually was to put together. Fake or not, they had my admiration for the sheer logistical nightmare managed.

Mom seemed collected enough, her response to the introductions to the judges professional and calm, though she smiled a great deal, and I was sure she was still quivering on the inside. When Patrice called for the first challenge to begin, some kind of cupcake thing I missed the details on thanks to my thoughts about the Reading treasure, she hurried to her kitchen with the precision and expression of a woman determined to win.

I caught myself holding my breath for the next hour, heart in my throat, hands fisted in my lap while I pleaded with anything and anyone out there to watch over Mom. I needn't have worried.

She moved through the challenge like a pro, not a single misstep slowing her down, even when Patrice approached her at the fifteen-minute mark to ask her questions.

I missed most of the conversation since I was at the edge of the set, but I caught a few words, mostly from my mother's perspective. She sounded awesome, smile brilliant but confident, as she finished her mix and slipped her cupcakes into the oven, spinning with a flare of her hem and apron to begin her icing.

By the time the last few minutes were counting down, Mom's force-cooled cupcakes were out of the fridge and almost complete, wrapped up her confections with a spiral of curved icing topped with tiny roses she'd constructed from some kind of edible gold leaf and sugar. I shook my head to myself, grinning. She'd done a fantastic job from what I could see, frustrating as it was to miss most of what was happening from this distance. Funny that I was sitting right here and yet I wouldn't get the full experience until I got to watch the episode.

That was TV for you, I guess.

I felt myself unclench as the timer went off, the hour of intense work over, the three women stepping back from the tray of cupcakes they'd constructed. For the first time, I checked out the other two and gasped softly to myself. Janet's were gorgeous, even from this distance, with elaborate toppers in multi-hued gardens cascading over the side of the icing. But Molly's were stunning, spun sugar spirals and leaves bursting from the centers of her shining white icing like crystalline towers of icy sweetness. I knew then Mom was out of her league, though I gave her kudos for the beautiful simplicity of her shining gold flowers.

She was first up, and though I knew she glanced at her competitors, she didn't lose a scrap of her outer confidence. I was so proud of her in that moment I could have burst, while the assistants rushed forward and placed her cupcakes in front of the judges.

The cameras rolling again, Patrice smiled at Mom, gesturing at her offering. "Lucy, can you tell us about your cupcakes?"

I didn't hear Mom's explanation, though I strained to catch every word. Why didn't Dale put me closer? So frustrating. From the way Mom talked, though, her soft hand gestures and the gentle smile on her face, she nailed her explanation. Even Vivian seemed grudgingly respectful of Mom's cupcake and, as the judges dug in, I wanted to be there, next to Mom, hugging her in her triumph.

Win or lose, the whole world would know just how delicious my mother's baking was.

They all took a bite at the same moment. Froze as they took their first chew. I knew something was wrong even before Olivia's face twisted, Vivian's whole body twitching. But it was Ron Williams spitting out the bite he took with a loud protest that clenched my stomach into a knot so tight I was sure I would never untie it.

Patrice's face flinched but she soldiered on, the camera still rolling. Why was the camera still rolling? Something had to be wrong. From the way Mom's confidence flickered, how her body tensed, this wasn't how things were supposed to go.

"Let's start with Olivia." Patrice looked desperate to get this over with. I caught sight of Clara gesturing in a circle to the camera operators, a clear signal to keep going.

Our mayor swallowed finally, forcing a smile past her obvious discomfort. "Ah, the cake is… moist. Very moist."

Vivian snorted, spitting hers into a napkin, setting it aside. "That's all it has going for it," she said. "I believe you were meant to use sugar as the main ingredient, Lucy. Not salt."

Wait, what? No. Mom would never make that mistake. That was the kind of switch I'd mess up. Besides, I saw Mom taste her batter. Didn't I? Wait, no. She never did. I watched that realization cross her face as Ron Williams coughed out the last of her cupcake and, red-faced, drew the full attention of everyone as well as the active cameras.

"Horrific and an assault on the senses," he rumbled, loud enough I heard him clearly from where I sat. Where I huddled, heart aching, watching Mom flinch from every single word delivered with cutting precision from a man she idolized. "I was expecting great things. Your form and design were mediocre at best, and the cake is a disaster. Honestly, whoever told you baking was your forte needs their head examined." His judgmental scowl deepened as he leaned toward her, jabbing at her with an index finger. "Go back to serving tables, if you can even manage such a task without ruining that simple job. Because this," he pointed aggressively down at the cupcake before him, "is why amateurs like you," another jabbed finger at Mom who actually rocked in place, the palest I'd ever seen her, "need to stay out of the kitchen."

Utter silence fell. Even I sat there, unable to move, gaping, unable to breathe, while my mother, my powerful and confident and amazing mother, burst into tears and ran from the set.

CHAPTER EIGHT

My first reaction after I watched my mother tear off the stage like she'd been handed her poor, shattered heart on a platter was the obvious. And before I could stop myself—who am I kidding? I had no desire to stop myself—I had stormed from my place on my stool at the fringe of the set and planted myself firmly in front of the three judges with, I'm positive, my rage showing on my face. Not aimed at Vivian, though she was a target later, nor at Olivia who fish-lipped at me like I'd broken about a dozen rules just showing up here. No, all of my animosity was aimed directly at the smirk on Ron Williams's face.

"How dare you." Not a question, not even a little bit of a care what he actually thought, honestly. "You arrogant, overblown, out of date—"

Dale appeared like magic at my elbow, hand on my arm, wincing. "This way, please."

I jerked myself out of his grasp, in no way willing to be escorted off just yet. I still had a plethora of insults to throw at the old gasbag perched on the stool on the other side of the counter like he was the boss of me and the rest of the planet. But when I opened my mouth to ramble on in suitable Fiona Fleming fired up fashion, I was interrupted yet again, this time by the red-faced Clara Clark.

"I thought I told you to get off my set." She spun on Crew of all people who'd joined me when I wasn't looking, his own scowl surely a match for mine. "You, local cop person. Take this, this," she stuttered a moment longer before finishing, "intruder off my sound stage!"

Well, I never. Instead of giving Crew the satisfaction of doing so, I spun and stormed off in the direction my mother had fled. Because I was so done with this farce of a ridiculous show.

The other side of the set led to a hallway, ending in an exit door. To the kitchen, I realized. Two more were visible, one an exit door at the far end and the other build into a box someone erected.

The green room Dale referenced, perhaps? I barged through the door, ready to murder if I had to, if that was what it took to rescue my mother from this injustice.

The space stood empty, couches lining the walls, coffee pot burbling, a small fridge beside it. I spun, still on adrenaline and fury, marching to the end of the hall and into the kitchen.

And found myself instead in the corridor that led to the staff quarters. I knew this place, suffered a bit of a shiver from the memory. I'd been pushed out the exit doors not too far from where I stood and into a snowstorm almost a year ago. I still had nightmares from the event, though they'd faded somewhat. Being here again surely meant I'd be revisiting the experience when I fell asleep that night, however.

Rather than allow myself to be distracted by my own fears, I instead headed for the one place I figured Mom might hide out at a time like this. The women's washroom door swung inward, and I immediately caught the sound of someone smothering sobs in one of the stalls.

The instant I set foot on the tile floor my heart, pounding with the anger of my need to support my mother, fell to the pit of my still knotted stomach. I'd only ever seen Mom cry with this much intensity twice in my life. The day I'd left for college and the first time I woke from being hit on the head last April. She'd done her best to hide it from me the first time, and I'd been in a terrible state of mind at eighteen, so I'd hardened myself against caring. I barely remembered my own name when Carter Melnick gave me a concussion, so Mom's tears weren't something I held onto last April, either. But this was different. Because these tears weren't about me. I knew how much she'd poured into this one giant effort and hearing her cry, knowing she was hiding from what happened, broke me.

I leaned against her door, forehead against the cool metal that protested softly from the pressure with a faint metallic hum. "Mom." I whispered that, unable to speak at normal volume, apparently. At least, until I cleared my throat, noting the thickness of it, how my eyes stung with my own unshed tears. Damn it, where was my anger when I needed it? Washed away with my mother's weeping. "Mom, are you okay?"

"Go away." Such a tiny protest, though about as clear a message as it could get.

"I'm not leaving you here, Mom," I said. That was better. Firm and decisive. "Open the door."

She didn't move, not a sound but her crying coming from the other side. I sighed, contemplated sliding under the door or trying to force the lock, when the main door slammed open, and Dad burst in.

I spun on him, anger returned. But before I could ask him just where he'd been all this time, he brushed past me, rattling the door to Mom's stall with a firm grip on the top.

"Lucy Fleming," he said, deep voice cracking. "Open this door right now. I'm taking you home."

I heard her move then, the faint click of her heels on the tile, the squeak of the lock turning. She pulled the door open, head down, refusing to look at either of us while the little shards of my heart shattered further into dust. I tried to hug her, but she brushed me off, hurrying past Dad and out the door while he glared after her before scowling down at me.

"This was a terrible idea," he said like it was my fault.

I could have started a fight. Didn't have the energy to spare. I had other intentions for my anger than yelling at Dad just yet. Instead, I let him go, marching after Mom, my own jaw bunching, teeth aching from grinding my molars together, hands fisted at my sides. I was going to go hunt down Ron Williams and punch him and to hell with the consequences. Right before I knocked Vivian and Olivia silly.

I'd just worked up enough steam to get moving again, my knees locked despite my need to stomp out and just smack someone already, when Crew's head popped into the bathroom, his blue eyes narrowing while he eased further inside, hands raising in front of him as if warding off some evil spirit. He had no idea.

"Fee." He sounded sad, though he looked stern. "Just let it go for now, please."

I shook my head, throat working, unable to speak. I needed to yell, to throw things, to act. But I couldn't. My whole body was frozen in place, the anger and sadness and disappointment for my poor mother making it impossible to control anything at the moment.

Probably just as well he showed up. Who knew what I'd have done if he hadn't?

"It's going to be okay," he said. "Olivia is on it.

She's livid about how Lucy was treated." I was sure there was more to it. She was probably pissed at me for interfering. Who cared? I certainly didn't. Crew's calm, empathetic demeanor did help unwind me from the tightrope of inaction holding me in place, unravelling the tension keeping me rooted in the spot.

I felt myself untangle and sag slightly, the tears returning. "Mom," I said.

"Your father took her home," Crew said, slowly coming to my side, one hand gently taking mine. I was surprised it didn't feel awkward, that his skin felt so warm and realized my own hands were icicles from clenching them tightly. "Let me escort you out, okay? We'll get this sorted and find out what happened."

I didn't care what happened, but I nodded rather than say that out loud and let him lead me to the door. He didn't let me go while he escorted me through the lobby. I stared at my feet, stumbling a little in reaction to what just happened, amazed that my need to protect Mom was so powerful it could render me this useless. I shook off the reaction as we hit the halfway point to the front doors, but held onto Crew's fingers anyway, squeezing faintly to thank him for his support.

I looked up as someone hurried to my side, exiting the dining room set. Dale bobbed a quick nod to Crew before shoving a small paper bag into my free hand. He didn't say a word, spinning and trotting back to the set, leaving me staring after him.

Crew got us moving again, out to my car, and, to my surprise, slipped into the passenger's seat while I opened the bag and peeked inside.

One of my mother's cupcakes sat there, slightly squished, the icing spreading on the side of the bag. I looked up into Crew's eyes and the two of us, without speaking, reached in and took a finger full.

I knew the moment it touched my tongue something horrible happened. Vivian was right. Mom used salt in place of sugar. But how could she have made such a huge mistake?

Crew's frown as he swallowed with a grimace deepened. Was he thinking the same thing as me? Apparently not, because while my mind spun over how Mom could have done something this wrong during such an important event, he spoke.

"Someone sabotaged your mother's baking," he said.

Fireworks shot off in my head, partly anger at myself for even considering Mom might have made a mistake, but mostly in realization he was absolutely right. I gasped in response, hand clenching around the cupcake.

"I asked Dale if the show was fair," I said. "I think he was going to warn me." I looked down at the cupcake. "He must have known. But why?" I was on the edge of crying all over again. "She's just a small-town woman with a wonderful heart. Why hurt her like this?" And why hadn't Mom tasted her batter?

Crew shook his head, hand on the door handle.

"I'm going to go ask some questions," he said. "You're okay to drive?" Those blue eyes, so full of concern. It was obvious, the way he looked at me, I'd misjudged how much I'd screwed up my chances. Either that or he was just a really good person who actually cared about other people and now I was overreacting in a wash of excessive emotion.

"I'll be fine," I said. "I need to see Mom." And let her taste this cupcake.

Crew hesitated a moment before nodding. "I'll let you know what I find out," he said before exiting the car, closing the door behind him. I watched him cross the snow-edged parking lot, my breath misting in the cold air and didn't start the engine until he disappeared inside the Lodge. Kicked myself I meant to say something, to tell him to come see me tomorrow night. Sighed over the lost opportunity but grateful this event at least seemed to have wiped the slate clean again. I decided to text him later, after I dealt with my mother's broken heart.

No fair the fluttering in my tummy over him had to come at such a high price.

CHAPTER NINE

Dad's truck and Mom's car were both in the driveway when I pulled up, so I knew they were home. I tucked my own car in behind Dad's to make sure I was off the street—stupid parking laws drove me nuts sometimes—and hoofed it to their front door. I didn't knock or slow down, barreling my way through and into the front entry. I did pause long enough to shed my boots, hopping and swearing softly under my breath as I tugged at the zippers and kicked them off sideways before sliding over the polished hardwood floor in my socks on my way to the kitchen.

Balancing the paper bag full of evidence in one hand.

Dad watched my progress with both eyebrows

raised over the rim of his coffee mug and for a moment I thought I'd overreacted. That Mom was totally fine, likely laughing over the whole thing herself. But when I came to a panting halt at the counter, my jacket hanging askew and my cheeks hot from the change in temperature, I realized there was no sign of her and that Dad was alone.

I tossed the bag down on the granite countertop, glaring at my father, wanting to yell at him for not being there for Mom but instead shoving the offending bag toward him. Dad set down his mug, all calm and whatever that stoically frustrating attitude of his actually was, before carefully opening the top of the paper bag and peeking inside. When he met my eyes again, he didn't seem any more upset than he had a moment ago.

"One of your mother's, I presume?" He didn't try to taste it, didn't lose his temper or ask me anything else. All good. I had the pissed off reactionary fireworks payload built up for the both of us.

"Someone sabotaged Mom's baking." I felt myself shudder when I said it, spitting the words out in hissing clips of syllables strung together like tiny arrows of accusation, choosing to trust Crew's assessment over my own judgmental first thoughts. "Where is she?"

Dad's gaze turned toward the hall beside him and their closed bedroom door. "I had that part figured out," he said, softer this time, sad at last. His reaction didn't lessen my anger any. If anything, his sorrow felt like acceptance and just fired me up further.

"What are we going to do about it?" I smacked the bag with the back of one hand, utterly offended by its presence now. "Does Mom know?"

"I told her what I thought," he said, shrugging faintly.

"Wow, nice effort, Dad." I snapped that at him before I could stop myself. "She doesn't need sympathy right now. She needs someone to go punch that asshole judge in the face." Okay, so my redheaded temper was getting the better of me. I had no idea I had this kind of protectiveness inside me, either. It startled me so much when it manifested, I actually stopped for a second and took a deep breath while Dad watched me with careful eyes.

"As much as I'd like to do just that," he said, "it won't do any good, Fee. We both know it. Aside from landing me in a jail cell. Something Crew Turner would find far too satisfying for my liking."

I grunted agreement. "Is she okay?" Yeah, there was my own empathy and sympathy, though I hated to let go of the burning rage that kept me moving and not crying for my mother. I'm sure she was doing more than enough of that she didn't need me adding to the tear fest.

Dad finally crumbled a bit, his hand shaking so much he had to set down his coffee mug and I realized in that moment his whole calm attitude was a façade. My father's typical reserved nature hid a wealth of emotion behind it, that much was clear, and I wondered then how much he'd masked over the years. How many times he'd felt so deeply but had been unable or unwilling to express it and how much damage that had done to him.

Dad's eyes met mine, tight around the edges, his Adam's apple bobbing slightly while he swallowed harder than usual. "I tried to talk to her," he said, choking up just enough I did, too. "I've never been good at this, Fee. I don't have the words." His hands spread before him like he offered me something but there was nothing there. "I'd never tell your mother not to do something that she wanted to do but, damn it. This time I wish I had stood my ground."

I nodded, looked away, my own hands digging deep into the pockets of my puffy coat while I struggled against tears. Okay then. Up to me, apparently. I shed my jacket, laying it on the counter—a chargeable offense if Mom had been here—and turned toward her bedroom door. Squared my shoulders, pulling on the anger I'd felt for her and marched down the hall.

She had to listen to me.

The door was locked, naturally. I wiggled the handle anyway, knowing it wouldn't do any good but needing her to know I was trying at least. "Mom."

I could hear her inside, ever so softly crying, like she was doing her best to hide it from both of us and maybe even from herself. "Go away, Fee." The repeated words from the Lodge bathroom didn't work here, either.

"Mom. I tasted your cupcake." I let that hang for a moment. "It wasn't your fault." I was positive of that. Thank you, Crew. "Mom, someone must have switched the sugar for salt."

Silence. And then thudding feet on the floor and the rattle of the door handle as she released the lock and jerked the door open. I took in her tear-stained face and her mottled complexion, the way her normally perfect hair was mussed and partially flattened, her makeup tracking down her cheeks. She looked frail to me, wasted, as if she'd given up the best of herself for that dumb show and they'd sucked her dry and left the remnants to blow away like a husk of my Lucy Fleming.

But anger burned in her green eyes as she snarled at me. "I didn't taste the batter," she said, like she'd murdered someone's puppy and liked it. "It's my own fault." She slammed the door in my face, locked it again and stomped away, leaving me to lean my forehead against the cool wood surface and sigh out my anger until all that remained was sorrow.

At least now I understood Dad's expression when I got here. It didn't matter if it was sabotage or not. Mom had already decided she was guilty of a crime someone else committed.

I returned to the kitchen, found Dad staring into his coffee. I retrieved the cupcake, dumped it firmly in the trash beside the counter and left, slipping on my jacket and hopping back into my boots, stumbling outside into the cold without a word. I finished zipping my coat in the front seat of my car, but it took me a long moment to turn the key in the ignition, to actually drive away, heading for home. How could I leave my mother in such a state?

As I pulled out into the street, a cargo van honked a warning. My stomach turned over, but not at the sight of the driver. No, it was the logo on the side that soured the bile in my middle. French's Handmade Bakery.

Vivian.

She'd been in the kitchen when I got there, had been wandering through all three of them. She could easily have made a label switch, couldn't she? Purposely sabotaged Mom's efforts to make herself look better. Hadn't she taken a smaller bite than the other two? Olivia's fork had been full, even Ron's was laden. Vivian had barely a quarter of a sliver. She knew not to eat too much.

I was going to kill her.

I spent the rest of my day fuming, pacing Petunia's with my faithful pug trailing after me. The Jones sisters avoided me after hearing about Mom's disaster. Turned out, actually, they already knew, the whole town did. Poor Mom. I was surprised when Daisy didn't show up and felt a zing of anger she wasn't here for me, for Mom. Not fair, and not like her, but I was on a jag and a roll, and no one was safe, good excuses or not.

By the time the sun set fully, the sky darkening across the mountains, I had worked myself into the kind of frenzy I recognized as inescapable. I could have tried to find a way to smother it, to pull back and examine my growing need to act in the kind of logical problem-solving breakdown I was sure most people employed to keep themselves out of trouble.

But to hell with that. I was done dodging my inner detective and if I'd learned anything from the past eighteen or so months living back here in Reading it was regardless of what happened around me, I always seemed to end up in the middle of it. So, why not make the choice rather than fall into it by accident?

I left Petunia behind, the quiet of the B&B's emptiness a relief, my January respite now an even bigger blessing. The pug whined at me as I closed the door in her face and hurried to my car, focus so intent I barely remembered the drive up the mountain or how I found myself striding around the outside of the Lodge toward the back door.

Thanks to Bill Saunders and his faithful Newfoundland dog, Moose, I'd learned the back way into the Lodge. Though I doubt the caretaker of the place ever expected me to break in like this. If anything, he'd showed me the way into the chair lift area only to make sure if I ever found myself trapped in the snow again I could get to safety. The lock on the door gave way to the key he'd secreted on the top of the ledge over it, and I slipped inside, letting the quiet darkness of the back hallway engulf me a moment.

Weird how I'd been here this morning, but it felt so different now. I'd been full of hope, optimism for Mom. Now? Now I just wanted to find the source of the sabotage and rub it in Vivian French's face. Of course, as I padded toward the side door to the dining room and the set, I was well aware finding evidence didn't mean Vivian did it. Or that she would confess even if I did turn up a mistake. I caught my breath as I pulled the door open and hovered on the threshold. What if I, instead, discovered Mom made a mistake and that it wasn't sabotage after all? What if it was Mom's fault?

I clenched my teeth as I let the door swing shut, scowling into the dimness of the back of the set, grateful it was quiet. I would never, ever tell my mother or anyone. A brief hit of insanity even informed me internally I'd switch the labels myself if I had to, just to protect Mom from any final assault on her confidence. As I crept toward the stage and her kitchen, the weight of the darkness punctuated by a few red glowing security lights, I told myself Mom came first.

Would I commit a crime for her? You betcha.

Except, as I crossed the stage to her area and bent to the shelf under her workstation, I knew what I'd find. The cover of the sugar was firmly in place, the faintest trace of flour on the edge of the rim visible in the low light. I twisted it free, stuck my nose in the glass jar and inhaled. The scent of sugar made me cringe. But wait. What was that ionized tang under it? I wet one finger, stuck it in the crystals and tasted the tip. Sugar, yes. Cut with enough salt it was no wonder her cupcakes were ruined.

I shouldn't have felt good about what I found, but the sigh of relief that escaped me made me dizzy and faintly nauseated. I sank to the floor, hugging the glass jar of evidence and stared up into the dark ceiling, thanking the Universe or the baking gods or whoever it was looked over me in that moment that this much, at least, was covered. Mom hadn't made a mistake. Except, of course, she hadn't tasted her batter. But that truth could be combatted. Especially with this fact in hand.

Now what? What exactly did I plan to do with the evidence, anyway? I tsked softly to myself, staring down into the white crystals. If it was Vivian, she'd just claim I was here to make her look guilty. I shouldn't have come alone. What was I thinking?

I spun the top back on and set the canister on the shelf, staring at it for a long moment before breaking out into a short fit of giggles. This was ridiculous, wasn't it? I'd broken into a film set to uncover a crime that really wasn't one. Unless a sodium overdose was an indictable offense? Sabotaging someone's cake batter was reprehensible, but it wasn't illegal. Heartbreak couldn't be converted to prison time, at least in this instance. Seriously, I'd lost all contact with reason and reality.

Speaking of which, this was a dumb, pathetic TV show that had zero bearing on the world as a whole. I would talk to Mom, make her see how silly this entire thing had been and help her thumb her nose at Ron Williams and this whole idiotic episode. In fact, it was time to do so right now. She'd listen, you better believe it.

I stood, turned toward the exit, shaking my head at myself, looking up as I headed for the way out again. And froze in place, heart stopping in my chest as I realized I wasn't alone. Someone sat at the judge's table, perched on one of the stools, watching me.

Busted. I hurried forward, mind spinning, wondering what to say when, for the second time, my poor, abused heart stuttered, jerked twice as it skidded over the truth and pounded back to regular rhythm while I came to a halt in the face of the truth.

Saying I wasn't alone? Not exactly accurate. While he was with me physically, tall, suited body slumped forward with a plastic bag tied tightly around his thick neck, the soul who had been Ron Williams was long, long gone.

CHAPTER TEN

I'd seen that look in Crew's eyes so many times it wasn't surprising anymore. But what was surprising? I no longer gave a crap how he judged me for stumbling over things that maybe I shouldn't have been involved in.

I finished telling him everything while I stood to one side, forcing my hands to stay calmly and quietly at my sides, chin up, voice level and steady while Dr. Aberstock checked out Ron's body, the paramedics waiting to transport the victim to the morgue. I purposely averted my eyes from what the doctor was doing because I didn't need to look.

Nope. I'd taken my time while I waited for Crew to arrive to do my own little examination—no touching, I swear—and was confident I'd come to the same cause of death Aberstock would. Asphyxiation wasn't a huge leap considering the circumstances I'd found Ron in.

"I'm not going to get into just how much trouble you're in right now." Crew's attempt to make me feel cowed and contrite was so far off the mark I had to bite my lower lip to keep from grinning. It was like he'd given up the effort, knowing it wouldn't do him a lick of good. Gone was his bullying anger, his disappointment even, replaced by a numb kind of acceptance. Cool, I was wearing him down. No, this wasn't funny, but surely, he knew better by now than to even try? That everything he said was kind of a waste of breath, no matter how it was delivered? I have no idea where the boost of gravitas came from or when I'd decided actively to just shrug off his attempts to keep me out of his business, but it happened and I was done arguing with my natural talent for curiosity satisfaction. He'd either have to arrest me for real or live with it.

I think he sensed my attitude shift long before he even tried to intimidate me because he sighed heavily before he tossed his hands, turning away from me so all I could see was his profile. Jaw jumping, cord in the side of his neck standing out. Typical Crew without the usual bossiness. I wondered if he was giving up on fighting me or me in general. That would suck but didn't change my mind.

"I should arrest you for trespassing," he said.

"You should find out why someone sabotaged Mom's cupcakes," I snapped.

Crew spun on me, brows low over his blue eyes as some of his anger returned. “You do realize how ridiculous that sounds. Or, on the other hand, how it makes your mother a suspect.”

Oh no, he did not just play that card on me. “You know,” I snapped, keeping my voice down though it was hard, so hard, not to yell at him, “you’d think you’d be over that kind of dumb ass reaction by now, Crew. That you’d know better than to accuse a Fleming of anything.”

There was the left eye twitch, awesome. “A man was murdered,” he said. “And yet again Fiona Fleming is in the middle of it. Maybe I should arrest you. God knows the town could use the break from violent crime.”

There was a time such an attempt to make me feel bad—clearly, a ploy to get me to back off, I could see that now—would have worked. Sent me scurrying back to Petunia’s to feel bad about myself before some evidence trail lured me out into the world again to find out things he should have uncovered himself.

Not this time. “So do it, Sheriff,” I said. “Or stop being an obtuse and arrogant jackass and listen to me for once.”

He looked like he was about to respond and likely in a way that would make both of us regret ever meeting each other. But Clara’s appearance ended that, followed by the hurried arrival of Janet and Molly. The only person who seemed to have his head on his shoulders was Dale. The young production assistant appeared at wits' end regardless, doing his best to corral the two stars before they could stumble into the crime scene.

Naturally, summoning Crew had lured out the showrunner. He'd likely called her, or hotel security had. Whatever the reason for her appearance, she made damned sure I was the least of Crew's worries at that moment.

"What the hell is going on?" She stared at the sight of Ron Williams being zipped into a body bag while Dr. Aberstock stepped back from the scene and let the two paramedics do their job. "Is that Ron?"

I spun on Clara personally, glaring at her while she met my eyes with her own scowl. She seemed rather low on the sorrowful scale and more irritated than anything. "He's been murdered." Crew grunted like I hit him, but I didn't let him interrupt. "And my mother's cupcakes were sabotaged." I jabbed a finger at the counter where the incriminating glass jar still rested. She could come to her own conclusions which I thought was the lesser of the crimes. "So, tell me, what kind of show are you running here?"

She tsked at me, rolling her eyes. "This is TV, kid," she said. "This crap happens all the time. Get over it." When she turned to Crew again, she blanched. "I meant the baking. Not murder. He was murdered?" Finally, her humanity started to show through, bleeding past the rigid and angry woman I'd met earlier today, again just now. "Who killed him?"

"Excellent question," I snapped, only to have

Crew's hand snake out and grasp my wrist. He didn't squeeze, barely touched me, but it was enough to silence me, his touch surprising in its gentleness.

"This is terrible." Molly appeared at my side, Janet next to Clara. They both stared as the paramedics rolled the body out of the room toward the lobby. I winced, thinking about Jared and Alicia and how having a corpse in their dining room wasn't going to be good for business. Considering this was their second murder in a year? Then again, death hadn't deterred tourists from Reading in the past, so who knew? Maybe it would be a good thing. Flinching from my line of truly inappropriate thought, I turned back toward Molly as she hugged herself and leaned into me. "Fee, how's Lucy?"

Wow, so kind of her to think of Mom at a time like this. Even though she was all I could think about. "Pissed," I said. "And Clara doesn't seem to give a crap." Well, considering someone just died, I should be cutting the woman slack. But, for all I knew, he'd died in part because of what happened to Mom, right? Sounded plausible.

Hey, don't judge me for putting my mother first.

"Seriously," Janet sniffed in my direction, pinched expression making her look like a shriveled apple. "A man is dead. Your mother's terrible baking is not the issue here."

Molly opened her mouth, frowning, looking like she wanted to protest when someone lunged from around Clara and attacked Janet. Can I be honest here? Just before I could.

"Cheater! Liar!" It took me a moment to realize it was Bonnie Williams. Fists flying, her long, dark hair whipping around her as she pummeled Janet in a fit of rage, the newly created widow of Ron Williams shrieked at the top of her lungs while the other woman shrank from her, forcing Crew to lunge between them and hold the attacker off. "You did this! You took him and took him and then you killed him because he didn't want you anymore." She sagged, words slurring as she staggered in Crew's grasp, sobbing then, almost falling and would have if he hadn't held her up.

Um, what was that? Before I could ask any questions, someone grasped my arm and tugged and I found myself being partly led, partly herded toward the exit. I fought against Dale's hand for a moment, but when Molly followed me, the two of them insistent with their expressions and their almost relentless retreat, I gave up and let them escort me out into the lobby.

The large space was abuzz with people gathered to talk about the death. It was still early enough in the evening to catch the attention of the guests, whispering as they stared out into the January night and the retreating ambulance. Word would get around town pretty quick that I'd found another body. Awesome. Didn't matter, not when I had two people in my presence I could grill for answers.

Molly beat me to speaking first. "I feel terrible for Lucy." Her long lashes blinked over her hazel eyes, her face pale, hands shaking as they took mine.

"Not for Ron?" Her sympathy wouldn't help Mom and I wasn't in the mood to accept it for my mother right now.

She flinched a bit, looked down, hands falling to tug her thin robe closed around her lean body. A bit early for bed, wasn't it, barely 6:45PM? Dale grasped her elbow as if he could support her with that simple touch.

"It's terrible, all of it." Molly spun away and ran for the elevators while Dale stared after her. Okay, pretty obvious he had feelings for her, but when he turned back to me, I could see the naked love in his eyes and refreshed my assessment accordingly.

"Ron Williams won't be missed," he said, then shook his head. "I'm sorry about Lucy, too, Fee. But not Ron. And I think you'll be hard-pressed to find anyone who misses him."

He spun and marched back into the dining room and, grim-faced, I followed. Only to be blocked by the one person who could keep me out as Deputy Jill Wagner emerged from the doors and planted herself on the lobby side, shaking her head at me with a firm but sad expression.

"Sorry, Fee," she said, shoulders bulky in her uniform jacket, no-nonsense blonde ponytail hanging over one shoulder. "Not tonight."

I ground my teeth together, crossing my arms over my chest. Jill was my friend, but she was also a deputy, and I knew asking her for help meant she'd put herself in trouble with Crew. If it had been my cousin, Robert Carlisle, I would have pushed past him and to hell with the consequences. Who was I kidding? A chance to get Robert in trouble? I'd have done it just to piss him off. But Jill was a whole other story.

Crew knew me too well already and we hadn't even had a date yet.

Fine, whatever. I spun without a word to her and marched for the front doors. I could still circle around and sneak back on set if I wanted to. Except there was nothing for me to do there, not right now. Maybe I could track down Dr. Aberstock? I stopped myself on the steps, breathing mist into the cold, clear night, shaking myself a little.

What was I doing and why? Mom needed me more than some dead judge who, it appeared, no one actually liked. I'd come here to prove her baking was sabotaged and I'd succeeded at that. While I might not have gotten any actual satisfaction from the parties involved, at least I knew now Mom hadn't made a mistake. As for Ron Williams's murder, it had nothing to do with me. I had a brief moment of headshake and resentment. Wished with a rush that made me shiver this whole dumb show idea had never happened and that Clara would pack up her horrible set and ridiculous fifteen minutes of fame offer and get out of my town.

Crew could have the murder. I was done.

But, as I descended to the parking lot at a clip, heading for my car, I couldn't miss the woman who hovered at the bottom of the stairs, staring off down the mountain. I hesitated beside her, caught her profile and recognized her as the woman Dale confronted earlier, the one who'd snuck onto the set much as I had.

My mouth opened, brain firing before my decision to walk away could kick in again.

"You're on the show?"

She turned her head, met my eyes, hers full of something I couldn't identify. But I finally put a name to her face, though she looked different than I remembered from TV. "Yes, I used to be." She sounded so sad and kind of broken. When she tried to walk down the last step she tripped. I reached out without thinking and caught her, helped her steady herself. Her weak smile triggered my curiosity and my empathy.

"Fiona Fleming." I tried a smile, surprised to find it came easily.

"Joyce Young." She seemed unable to stop herself from looking back down the mountain, in the direction the ambulance went. "Last season's runner-up."

Yes, she was indeed. "What are you doing here?" Because that was my business.

She didn't seem to mind the question, though she answered it with one of her own. "Is he…" she swallowed hard. "Is he dead?"

I nodded, not sure what to say. Even as Joyce turned to me, caught my affirmative and burst into tears.

"Thank god," she whispered and ran off.

CHAPTER ELEVEN

I should have run after her, chased her down, asked her why she reacted the way she did to the death of Ron Williams. She'd been runner-up in the show last year. Did she have hard feelings about him and her loss? I'd seen firsthand how horribly he treated people who didn't live up to his standards. But then there was the Bonnie attack on Janet and the clear to me now implication that maybe Ron wasn't so faithful to his wife.

Did that mean Joyce had a history with Ron that could make her a suspect in his murder?

Voices behind me turned me around, my attention caught by Crew and Jill as the two exited the front doors. Without thinking—my favorite—I retraced my steps and joined them. Jill seemed startled by my appearance, ducked out about a second before Crew realized I was there. The look on his face gave me pause and made me wonder if my timing could be worse or if I should just turn around and go back to my car without my typical blurting to put distance between him and me.

Instead, I spoke up, because yeah. "You need to talk to Joyce Young," I said.

"You need to mind your own business." Crew said it like it had become rote to him, a saying he wished I'd finally get through my thick skull. Not happening.

"You don't understand," I said, spluttering as I turned and gestured in the direction the woman ran off into the darkness. She must still be on the property. He could catch up with her easily.

Crew settled one hand on my shoulder and attempted to push me down the stairs. Okay, that sounded worse than it was. He didn't try to kill me or anything. At least, I didn't think so. But he was certainly taking liberties, manhandling me like that. I jerked away from his touch, scowling at him for the attempt. To his credit he backed off, letting his hand fall to slip into the pocket of his jacket, though he looked about as grim as a block of stone carved from the mountain around us as he spoke.

"No, Fee," he said, "I don't think you understand." So cold, that tone. Uncalled for. "I wasn't kidding in there. About Lucy. You seem to think you and your family are insulated from the law, that you have some kind of free rein over this town."

He said what? "But I'm here to let you know I'll be talking with your mother in short order, likely in the next hour or so. Just in case you want to warn her ahead of time. So she can get her story straight." He didn't sound like he was trying to be helpful.

Jerk, how dared he? "If you think for one second I'm going to let you bully my mother because you're having a rough night, you've got another thing coming." Did he. Like my foot up his very shapely behind. Cute or not, like him or not, if he tried to pin this on Mom, he was a dead man. He could come after me all he wanted, had, in fact, when Pete Wilkins died. Even came for Dad. But Mom? Yeah, they'd find his corpse floating in the lake before I'd let him near my mother.

Growl.

"Ron Williams died after humiliating your mother in public," Crew snapped then, nose inches from mine, the scent of coffee on his breath reaching me as the mist of his exhale washed over my face. "Suffocated with an empty bag that her show apron was wrapped in." Wait, I didn't know that. "Sounds like motive and means to me."

I'd give him motive. "You really think she'd be that stupid?" Seriously. "You're just trying to punish me for finding another damned body in this freaking ridiculous town." I thought we'd gotten this out in the open in October. None of the bodies I'd encountered had been my fault. "And before you ask, smartass, I didn't kill him. Would have loved to choke him on a handful of the cupcake my mother baked after whoever sabotaged her chances broke her heart. Because I can tell you one thing." I shook my finger in his face while his nostrils flared, pupils dilating as his temper rose. "If I was going to kill Ron Williams, you'd know it was me. As for Mom, she's an expert marksman. And smart enough to kill with a bullet from a distance."

Okay, I was exaggerating. Um, outright lying? Mom hated guns, always had. The one time Dad took her to the firing range she'd been so shaken by the explosion of the pair of small blocks shaped like rabbits I thought she was going to fall over. Besides, defending Mom by saying she was capable of murder by single bullet? I wasn't sure that was exactly a rousing cry of innocence. Did make me think of my father in the heartbeat between my ridiculous statement and what I planned to tell him he could do with his accusations. Could Dad have…? Maybe if Mom was physically hurt in some way. But over cupcakes?

"Are you done?" Crew waited for me to nod. I took my time. Just because. Watched the tic under his eye dance and the irritation on his face that he saw me notice. "Last time I'll tell you this, Fee. Go home. And stay out of it."

It was so tempting to stick my tongue out at him in that instant. The most childish of reactions, I could barely hold it in. Instead, I tossed my head, my red hair swirling behind me in what I told myself was a majestic flow of auburn mane before striding for my car. Slipped twice on patches of ice that utterly ruined my queenly exit, but whatever.

I was only home for five minutes, long enough to bundle on another scarf and stuff Petunia's rotundness into a harness and protective shoes before I exited the B&B again and hurried to Mom's. I could have taken my car, but I needed the physical outlet and a brisk walk in the chill of the January evening did a lot to cool my temper, much more than the annoyed and sniping drive I took down the mountain, telling Crew off in my head to the point if he'd shown up in front of me, I'd have run him over.

By the time Petunia clattered up the walkway to Mom and Dad's, her little booties tapping on the cold pavement, I had a handle on my anger and a plan. At least, I told myself that when I knocked on the door before letting myself in.

Petunia bounded away from me, heading for the kitchen when I unhooked her harness, her boots sliding over the hardwood floor with a squeaking sound. I heard Mom say her name and hurried to join my pug, finding my mother sitting on the floor with her back against the stove, Petunia in her lap eagerly licking tears from her cheeks.

I stood there a long moment and stared down at Mom, wishing I could help but knowing Petunia was doing a far better job than I ever could. By the time my mother released the pug from her hug, the wiggling dog chatting with her over her excitement in seeing her, Mom was at least no longer crying openly.

She looked up, caught my eyes, dropped her gaze quickly. "You didn't have to come back."

"I did." I sank to the floor across from her, squeezing one of her feet. All of the anger ran out of me, leaving me feeling deflated and tired. "Mom, I went back to the set. I checked the sugar." She sniffed softly, stroking Petunia's ears. "I was right. I tasted it. Mom, someone cut it with salt."

She finally met my eyes again, a faint bit of her own anger rising before it died. I watched it snuff itself out while she wiped at her nose with the back of her hand.

"It doesn't matter, Fee," she said. "I should have tasted my batter."

She'd be using that punishment against herself for a long time unless I could change her mind.

"Since when do you expect your best recipe that you've made a million times and tested every single time to need testing again?" I wished I could fix this for her, but she had to come to forgive herself on her own. I saw it as she cringed from my attempt to make her feel better. "Mom."

"Always test your batter." A life lesson? "It doesn't matter anyway." Was she getting over it? That would be awesome. Except, the bright and bubbly woman I knew wasn't coming back, hadn't bounced out of her funk just yet. I guess she earned a bit of angst, and her defeat had only come this morning. Still.

"Mom," I said. Stopped. Telling her what happened might piss her off. Then again, being angry with me for finding yet another body could snap her out of her sadness. Still, she'd been so upset with me in October when I'd gotten tangled in Sadie's murder, I wasn't sure spilling what happened tonight was a good idea. Except, of course, Crew was going to come and question her, and she'd be finding out anyway. Best to get the mess direct from the horse.

She looked up when I didn't finish right away. "It's okay," she said. "You don't have to stay."

"That's not it." I groaned and sagged back, Petunia leaving her and coming to me before snuffling Mom's pristine floor for crumbs. "Ron Williams was murdered."

Mom gasped, both hands going to her mouth, bloodshot eyes huge. "What happened?" I told her, wincing as I admitted I found him. Despite my initial nervousness, I needn't have worried. Mom patted my knee before sinking back against the stove again, shaking her head.

"How horrible," she said, hiccupping softly. "For you, honey." Her eyes narrowed. "Not him."

Yikes. Well, if she wanted to hate him where once she adored him, awesome, I was all for it. Except, of course, he was dead and that kind of attitude in front of Crew would get her a nice, warm jail cell and a murder charge. "Where were you tonight?" I knew better than to ask, but she had to understand what was coming.

Mom shrugged, casual and uncaring. "Here," she said. "Baking. Trying to figure out what I did wrong." Her shaking hands rose a moment then fell into her lap. "Silly. I knew in my heart it wasn't me, Fee. But I couldn't help myself." This time a tiny sob rose, one she smothered with a fist over her lips.

I looked around then, anger reappearing. "Where's Dad?"

She shook her head. "I don't know. I took a nap and when I got up, John was gone. So, I started baking." Petunia seemed to have found some trace of what Mom was making earlier and got busy snorfling it in the corner. Not like Mom to leave a mess, but then again, she wasn't exactly herself right now.

Meanwhile, my heart hurt. How could he leave Mom alone at a time like this? Yikes. I'd suspected Dad of murder once before, of killing Pete Wilkins. Could he have killed Ron? But no, Dad would never do anything to point the finger at Mom. Like me, if she wanted the guy dead, he'd be dead. But if Dad did it? No one would ever find the body.

"Fee." Mom swallowed hard, staring at her hands in her lap. "There was a controversy last season. One of the contestants claimed she was sabotaged, and she lost because of it. It was a huge scandal the show swept under the rug."

I stared at her a long moment but didn't see her. Not when the face of Joyce Young swam in my head.

"The contestant accused Janet of cheating." Mom cleared her throat before going on. "But Ron backed her and the other woman lost. Someone said she was paid off to shut her up and the mess increased ratings."

"You knew the show was rigged," I said. "Why did you enter?" Oh Fee, way to hurt your mother.

Instead, Mom shrugged, voice tiny as she

answered. "I didn't believe it. I thought she was lying. I wanted to think Ron was a good person." She stilled. "I was wrong. About so many things."

I exhaled into the quiet of my mother's dark kitchen, my pug finally finishing her hunt for extra morsels and collapsing between us, groaning softly in the stillness while I wondered about our screwed-up culture and how much stock we put into total strangers we thought we knew because we saw them on television every week.

"I know you think I'm pathetic," Mom said, wiping at her nose again absently. "I'm a grown woman. It's a stupid cooking show. I shouldn't have believed I even had a chance. Or that I should expect to be treated fairly. But I did, Fee." She finally met my gaze again. "I really did. Now I don't know what to do or how to feel about myself."

My lower lip trembled as I slid toward her, trying to hug her. She dodged me but I wasn't going to let her escape a giant Fee hug, not right now, not when she needed it the most. Except, naturally, at that instant, the doorbell rang, and I promised myself I'd punish whoever stood on the other side for giving Mom the excuse to escape me.

Just before she reached the entry, I called out to her. "Mom, what was the contestant's name? The one who accused Janet?"

"Joyce Young," she said, and opened the door.

Of course, it was.

CHAPTER TWELVE

I scowled at Crew when Mom let him in, as he took off his fur hat and nodded to my mother, voice low but carrying.

"Evening, Lucy," he said, glancing up when Petunia waddled to greet him, then to me before he met Mom's eyes again. "I'm sorry to bother you. Fee's told you about the murder?" Mom nodded. "You'll understand then why I have some questions?"

I wanted to be mad at him, but his tone was careful, kind, respectful. So, I didn't say anything when Mom gestured for him to enter. He even took a moment to slip out of his boots, to scratch Petunia behind her ears as she moaned her happy pug pleasure at his touch. When he joined us at last, sock feet sliding over the polished hardwood, jacket zipper humming when he undid it, I did my best not to cut him any slack for what he was about to do. His job, but still.

Still.

"Is John home?" Crew didn't look around, kept his gaze on Mom. Too compassionate, too gentle. I wanted to be furious with him and instead, I found myself mentally begging him to just get it over with.

"No." Mom's pale cheeks pinked faintly. "I know what you're here to ask and I can assure you neither of us had anything to do with Ron Williams's passing."

Crew's gaze flickered to me and back to Mom. "You of all people know I have to do this, Lucy. To eliminate you."

Her normally gracious nature was nowhere in sight. She turned sideways, away from him, arms crossing over her chest, chin tilting upward as her face set into a mask of blankness.

"John's right," she snapped. "You're a young fool without the sense the maker gave you. Ask your damned questions and then get out of my house."

Wow. I'd never seen Mom act like this before. Bitter and resentful and not herself at all. Wasn't letting Crew off the hook, though. Because he could have left, apologized and done this later. Instead, he gritted his teeth visibly, jaw jumping, and forged on.

"Where have you been since the taping ended?" Nice way of saying since she ran off the set in a mess of tears.

"She's been here," I snapped.

"I didn't ask you," he said. Inhaled. Exhaled. "Lucy? Have you been home?"

Mom flinched, not out of guilt, I was sure of that, but because I could see her face, while he only had her profile. Watched the self-condemnation travel over her features when she clearly relived her exodus from the Lodge earlier in her mind. This wasn't happening, not on my watch.

"I told you already." I stepped between him and Mom. "You know, I think my mother is too tired for your questions and maybe she wants to talk to a lawyer before she says anything further, Sheriff."

Crew's temper made an appearance. At least he saved it for me and didn't use it on Mom. "Does she need a lawyer, Fee? Something I don't know about?"

"I think everyone who comes in contact with you in this town needs a lawyer at some point," I snapped back. "Because you obviously have zero idea how to investigate a real crime or you'd be out there talking to the people who worked with and were screwed over by Ron Williams."

Oopsie doodle. I watched his own brand of doubt cross his face before he slammed it down again.

"I'm doing my job," he said, quiet, controlled. "I'm questioning people connected to the victim. It's called police work, Fee. Something you don't understand because you never went to the academy. Instead, you prefer to bumble around and make everyone's lives miserable, preferably mine, from what I can tell."

"If that means keeping you away from my mother when she had nothing to do with the murder you should be out there investigating," I said, "then so be it."

"Oh, would you two just stop it!" Mom startled me, startled both of us. I spun to find her cheeks wet with tears, dark red with building emotion, hands wringing in front of her. "Just stop it and go away and leave me alone!" I watched her run from the room, down the hall, the sound of her footfalls ending at the slamming of her bedroom door.

Petunia's whine and a wash of icy air was the only warning we had we weren't alone anymore, that we'd had a witness to Mom's outburst, unexpected and terribly timed. For Crew, that was. I turned to find Dad standing in the entry, looking about fit to tear the sheriff in half, glaring as he slammed that door, just as Mom had hers, towering over both of us like a bear who'd been poked one too many times with a very sharp stick.

"What's going on?" Dad stomped toward us, not bothering to take off his boots. A small part of my mind winced that Mom would be furious with him for tracking the world outside onto her clean floor while Crew stiffened beside me.

"I had questions for Lucy," he said, all professional again, "and I have some for you."

"I heard." Dad wasn't in the mood, apparently. "We'll be by the station in the morning. But right now, Crew, you're no longer welcome in my house.

Not if you insist on making my wife cry." He paused on his way past both of us. "In case you missed it, she had a bad day. You know very well Lucy didn't kill that judge and putting her through this right now is just petty." Crew actually flinched next to me. "You've got a lot to learn yet about being sheriff in a small town." Dad swallowed, anger fading while he walked away, his parting words carrying over his shoulder. "You want to make sure this job stays yours? A bit of compassion never hurt anyone, young man."

I had no idea what Dad's comment about Crew keeping his job meant, but I didn't really care just then. Dad left, finally shedding his boots at the threshold of the kitchen, leaving us both there, Petunia panting between us, and disappeared down the hall toward the bedroom and Mom. Never mind he was in a whole heap of trouble for leaving her alone in the first place. But I'd deal with that later.

I spun away from Crew and headed for the exit, hating how much time it was going to take to get away from him, feeling the burn of tears in my eyes, the tightness in my throat. Why couldn't it be summer? I could slip-on sandals and race out the door. Instead, I grunted my way into my boots before snapping on Petunia's lead, grateful I hadn't taken off her foot protection, looking up at last to find Crew standing there, his own boots firmly in place, hands in his pockets, expecting it to be awkward.

Instead, his blue eyes were so sad I faltered,

paused. Waited for him to say something despite wanting to run away.

"If you could just…" he gestured for me to make room. Ah. He wasn't being polite. I was in his way. I grunted at him before stepping aside, staring down at Petunia who whined softly at me, as if sensing I was unhappy and not sure how to fix the problem. If only she could.

Crew didn't try to leave, though he did close the gap between us, hovering with one hand on the door handle.

"Did he suffocate?" Because asking about the case felt better than trying to figure out why the distance between Crew and me felt as vast as a chasm instead of a bare few inches in a small entry.

He nodded without argument. "Right before you found him. Doc said he'd been dead less than a half-hour."

Creepy. I'd arrived at about 6PM. Had I been entering the set when he'd been struggling for his last breath through the thick plastic over his face? Queasiness turned my stomach, but I wasn't here to defend myself.

"Mom's awfully small to wrestle such a big man and hold him down long enough to smother him with a plastic bag." Not quite an accusation.

"Doc thinks he was struck from behind, was unconscious before the bag was applied." Crew gave that up without a hint of hesitation. "Someone whacked him with a pot. I found it in the trash with a big dent in it. Fee, the only one missing was from your mother's kitchen."

"Yet another reason not to suspect her," I said. Because obvious did not become a former sheriff's wife.

He sighed. Nodded. "I know," he said. "But I have to do my job." Again with shoving that fact between us. I wondered about what Dad said. Was Crew in trouble over how he ran things? He left without another word while I shivered in the cold he let in, knowing that shudder reaction had more to do with the regret in his voice than the January night.

CHAPTER THIRTEEN

I almost turned around and went back into the house, to confront Dad and try to comfort Mom again. Instead, tired and knowing I could only make things worse, I headed out the door, Petunia tugging on the leash, eager to go home. I kind of agreed with her.

I made it to the street before I realized Crew hadn't left yet and flushed while I stopped in surprise, my pug happy enough to pause and wait for me to do something besides gape at him sitting behind the wheel of his truck, staring into the dark.

I could have kept walking. After all, he'd done it to me, exited Mom and Dad's and gave me an out. But I had two important things to tell him and while I knew I ran the risk of setting him off all over again

I also couldn't in good conscience let them go.

My mittened knuckles knocked on the glass and made him jump. Honestly, I'd just seen him. Why did he look so surprised to find me standing there? He wound down his window, blue eyes startled and open as I nodded to him, letting him see I wasn't angry but determined.

"Two things and I'm out," I said. "Look into Joyce Young if you haven't already. She lost last year and accused Janet of cheating. Ron sided with her. She was at the Lodge today."

Crew didn't flinch or look pissed so I rushed on.

"And I saw Malcolm Murray leaving the set," I said. "I have no idea if he's connected, but he and his boys were there for a reason, so he might have a history with someone there." I stepped back from the open window, shivering in the cold. "There. That's it. I'm done."

"Fee, I'm sorry about Lucy." Did he hear what I just told him? "That was… horrible. She deserves so much better." Did he mean just now, tonight, or at the show? Didn't matter. He looked truly regretful, upset. "She's a really great person. I hope she's okay."

I cleared my throat because I wasn't going to break down and cry on the sidewalk in front of Crew. Not happening.

"She'll be fine," I said, knowing it sounded forced, before sighing into the darkness. "This is just terrible timing for her. She's under a lot of pressure with the wedding coming. And Vivian's been pretty nasty about Mom taking on the job." Crew didn't seem surprised by that. "The last thing she needed was a hit like this. I think she's been struggling with confidence." Yikes, way to stab your mother in the back like that, Fee. But where else did this burning need to prove herself come from? I knew I was right, that I'd been trying to ignore the truth of the matter since Mom told me about Aundrea and Pamela's upcoming wedding. Since Vivian's secret conversation with Mom in October, the details of which I still hadn't heard. I'd warned the Queen of Wheat off, but that didn't solve the initial issue.

Was my amazing, strong and talented mother suffering a crisis of personal faith?

"I have nothing but respect for Lucy," Crew said. "I want you to know that, Fee. She's been so kind and welcoming when not everyone was." This was news. "But she made sure I knew I had her support from the day I arrived." I didn't know that, either. Huh. "It meant a lot to me." His hands grasped the steering wheel as if doing so gave him the courage to speak. "I wasn't sure I'd made the right decision. I knew when I took the job your father was well-loved and had been sheriff a long time. But when I showed up that first day and your mother was in my office with a basket of fresh baking and a hug… well. I wasn't expecting that." He licked his lips, finally met my eyes again. "And knowing I hurt her just now, that doesn't sit well with me. There's no excuse, regardless of what my job demands."

I gaped at him. I had zero clue Mom did such a

thing, but you know what? That was Lucy Fleming. All class, all the time. I could just see her and her beaming smile, her eager embrace, how firm and friendly she'd have been with him. Making sure he was at ease in his new job. More tears threatened. She was my hero.

Crew glanced down at Petunia, then up at me while I swallowed past my burning throat. "It's pretty cold," he said. "Did you two ladies need a ride home?"

I almost said no, that we were fine. But I was far more tired than I thought and when he stepped out of the truck and hoisted Petunia into his arms, I relented.

While the cab wasn't warm, it was better than being out in the chill. The wind had begun to pick up, dropping the temperature rapidly. The walk to Mom and Dad's had been heated with anger. The return trip, minus the fiery impetus of my need to fix my mother would have been rather miserable. I clicked on my seatbelt, the pug seated jauntily between us, her butt rounded under, hind legs poking out beneath her like a toddler while Crew fired up the truck and pulled out.

It was a short drive, made longer by the fact he had to circle the block, but not much. So weird, I actually felt nervous, a bit trembly, waiting for the other shoe to drop. All the bubbling anxiety I felt around him when I noticed he was a deliciously yumtastic chunk of manliness came back in a rush and I found I was overheated despite the winter weather.

Of course, he had to ruin it. Usually my job, so fair enough he got to take a turn.

"Fee, I know this is terrible timing, but I need to ask." That private something he wanted to talk to me about? I waited and he went on in a rush. "Is your father up to something?"

Maybe he didn't mean it to sound like an accusation and perhaps it was, indeed, an icebreaker rather than a confrontation starter. He'd prepared me with a caveat after all. But considering the expectation I had of a more intimate question and the relationship we had, he had to know the second it left his mouth what kind of reaction his question would get.

I refused to acknowledge his faint flinch, his knowing frown because it was clear he did understand he'd stuck his foot in it. Didn't keep me from the sharp jab of anger, though.

"That's why you offered me a ride, is it?" I hugged Petunia to me, the pug protesting softly but snuggling after a second. "I have no idea what you're talking about." Then again, I'd noticed it too. Where was Dad this morning when Mom needed him? And tonight? Why did I find her alone? Not to mention his connection to Malcolm. Crew knew about that connection because I'd asked him about Dad and the Irishman earlier. But if he thought I was going to throw Dad under the bus in favor of giving Crew information against my own father? Even if I had it. Which I didn't.

I had to look up that woman's name. Siobhan Doyle could give me the answers, I was sure of that. But did I really want to know? Part of my anger at Crew was anger with myself for being an idiot and not doing the research, for being a coward. Didn't stop me from letting him bear the brunt of it the rest of the decidedly chilly drive to Petunia's.

Good thing it was only a couple of blocks because the tension in the truck was so heated by the time he pulled to a stop by my front door I was positive one more second of it would have led to spontaneous combustion. I fumbled with my seatbelt, hating that my anger always made me clumsy, jerking on Petunia's leash and finally slamming my way out of the cab, the pug grumbling at my feet. Crew pulled away without another word as I stood on the sidewalk and glared after him, just barely resisting the urge to flash him my middle finger.

Might have hidden the act in my pocket.

I stomped up the steps and into the foyer, Petunia flinching from me to the point I had to pull myself together so she didn't stare up at me like that with those big eyes full of hurt. I crouched and hugged her, wishing I could have had the chance to do the same to Mom, looking up to realize I wasn't alone. Or the only source of angst in the world.

Daisy stood in the middle of the entry, a vaguely terrified smile on her face while on one side Joyce Young hovered, pinched and pale but unrelenting and Bonnie Williams glared on the other.

CHAPTER FOURTEEN

"Fee!" Daisy's desperate blurting of my name told me everything I needed to know, even if I'd been blind to the animosity between the widow and the woman who hovered, nervous but angry, as if waiting for a hit that didn't come.

I was actually grateful for the as yet unexplained source of the pending confrontation about to unfold in front of me, taking the opportunity to use it to help pull myself under some semblance of not a crazy lady. At least, in comparison to the pair of women who faced off in my foyer.

"Mrs. Williams." I swept forward, taking Bonnie's arm and guiding her into the kitchen, Petunia trailing behind me. I glanced over my shoulder to see Daisy doing the same for Joyce but in the other direction, leading her to the stairs with a grateful nod and smile. I didn't stop moving until I had Bonnie seated at the kitchen counter with a cup and saucer in front of her and a pot of tea brewing, taking her coat and laying it over the back of a stool while Petunia sat at her feet in her cute harness and booties.

"I just couldn't stand to stay in that place any longer." Bonnie's hands trembled as she clasped them in front of her on my counter, gaze haunted and lost. She hiccupped faintly, swaying on her stool, but caught herself before she spoke again. "Not in the same room Ron and I… I…" she sobbed once before looking away, lips a thin line, hugging herself.

I sat beside her, poured tea, all too familiar with this particular scene and, oddly, at ease because I'd handled grief in varying forms and degrees with a pot of my favorite blend before.

"I'm so sorry for your loss, Mrs. Williams," I said. "You must be devastated."

She leaned toward me then, took my hand. "I'm sorry," she whispered, broken through her tears. Was that wine on her breath? Would explain the glaze in her eyes, her condition when she attacked Janet earlier. That meant she'd been drinking in the afternoon. Was that typical of her? "The way Ron treated your mother. She's a darling, from what I know of her. So kind how she gushed over me when we met. No one else seems to notice me, but she knew who I was right off." She had the faintest British accent, and it came through in the way she spoke, though I could guess she hadn't lived overseas in many years. "She spoke so highly of Ron and the show."

That was my mom, making everyone else feel special and at ease. Who did that for her? Time for her daughter to step up, right?

"My mother is an amazing woman," I said, "and I'm so lucky to have her." There I went, choking up again. "She's also an incredible baker. I was stunned when her work didn't turn out."

Bonnie flinched, shook her head, poking at her now red nose with a bit of used tissue. I fetched her a fresh one and she sparked a bit of a smile in response, tugging at the lines on her narrow face. "He was utterly wretched to her, and I told him so. He's such a beast. Was." She exhaled. "I guess I'll have to get used to the past tense."

I nodded. "You were close, I take it? You're on the set quite a bit?"

Bonnie didn't hesitate, though she slurred enough in her speech I could tell she was still over the legal limit. "Not at all," she said. "He was a cheating bastard who had affairs with all his favorites, including Janet." She scowled then like a switch had flipped inside her, from sorrow to rage as she glared over her shoulder at the kitchen door. "And that trollop, Joyce Young."

Now I had the rest of the story. I gaped at her, unable to speak, certainly the last thing I expected to come out of her mouth despite knowing there was something between her and Joyce. She smiled again, patting my hand, sipping her tea as if nothing untoward happened just now. Like revealing she shared a roof presently with one of her husband's mistresses.

"It's all right, dear," she said. "It's old news. Anyone close to the show would tell you the same thing. I hated him sometimes, but he was my husband." She shrugged. "I'm sorrier for how it happened, that it will hurt the show. Especially since his death could mean it will be canceled now."

"Why does that make you sad?" I barely registered I managed a question.

"Why," she seemed surprised by my words, "because I have a lot of money invested in it, dear. I stand to lose a great deal of capital if it goes under."

So she said. I had no compunctions, as her grief seemed to fade in the light of the truth, about thinking of her as a murder suspect.

"What about Molly Abbott?" I didn't fill in the blanks of the question, though I was sure Bonnie knew what I was asking. I hoped for the best. I couldn't see the sweet young woman as one of Ron's conquests. When Bonnie shook her head, lips twisting, I had my confirmation.

"That one has a head on her shoulders," she assured me. "Delightful young woman, going places. When this is settled, I might talk to her about her own show."

Blink and miss it, apparently. She was moving way too fast for me, or maybe it was the wine I could only assume still raced through her veins if the continuing smell on her breath was any indication. I was accustomed to grieving widows and mothers, hurt and aching battered wives, even heartbroken women who had the love of their life torn from them because they weren't the right gender in the eyes of their family. But this?

I was not expecting this.

"Well, I suppose this saves me having to file for divorce." Bonnie sighed into her cup. "My lawyer will be horribly disappointed he's missing out on billable hours, but it does simplify things."

"Wow," I whispered.

She tilted her head to one side, tsking. "I know, right? So much drama resolved with a single death. Now, if only we can salvage the rest of the season. Perhaps a guest judge or two." Her lower lip trembled again. "I just don't know what I'll do if I lose profit on this venture." She sobbed into her tissue while I gaped at her and tried to find something to say.

Inappropriate? Check. Her first.

"Why didn't you file for divorce ages ago?" If she was going to be all logical and practical, I figured a bit of inappropriate wasn't too far off the path.

She sniffed into her tissue. "Money, of course. Honestly, dear, you don't understand this business at all, do you?" She did not just condescend me. "The more he made, the more I could take him for when it was over, not to mention my profits from the show itself. Besides, he was prepping to launch that ridiculous new cookbook of his. It's already poised for the New York Times bestseller list. Far too lucrative to pass over."

"Right," I said. "Of course. How silly and financially irresponsible of me."

She waved the tissue at me, wrinkling her nose like she smelled something funny. Maybe the stench of alcohol was getting to her like it was to me. "He was going to launch on the show, end of season. It meant a chance at endorsements and even a bigger judging position, even a show of his own." She sipped her tea, blowing on the steam rising from the delicate china of my grandmother's cup. "I was just being practical."

"Utterly," I said, unable to muster much enthusiasm. She didn't sense it, apparently, because she smiled like I understood her better than her own mother. "Sounds like you're going to get everything now?"

Bonnie shrugged, simpered, then frowned. "So much potential wasted."

Holy crap. That was cold, even for someone under the influence. "Has the sheriff spoken to you about your whereabouts tonight?" I assumed as much, and since the spouse was often a suspect, I had to guess Crew had her on his radar.

Turned out that was the wrong thing to say. She huffed at me, setting the cup down a bit too solidly, the tinkle of china making me wince she might have broken something.

"Honestly," she said. "That young man and his questions. He's part of the reason I left the hotel in the first place." She stood then, wavered on her heels, turning as Daisy appeared at the kitchen door. "Perhaps your help could escort me to my room? I'm suddenly feeling peaked and need to lie down."

I just bet she was feeling something, and it had nothing to do with her husband's murder and everything to do with how much she'd had to drink today. I didn't respond with such insulting thoughts, though, letting Daisy lead her out, raising my eyebrows at my best friend who rolled hers back behind the woman's arrogant and somewhat wobbling departure. A quick check of the cup showed a tiny sliver of the base had chipped free. I sighed over the damage, hoping a bit of glue could salvage the break, wishing life was as easy to fix.

CHAPTER FIFTEEN

Daisy returned and joined me for a cup of tea herself, her huge, gray eyes wide when I filled her in on what happened all day. She shook her head in horror, hand over her mouth, when I told her about Mom and grasped my wrist when I was done, tears standing in her gaze.

"Fee, I'm so sorry." Her voice trembled when she spoke. "I got a call from Rose late last night. I had to drive to Montpelier to help her." She flushed as I frowned at her.

"Rose?" I had nothing. Who was Rose?

Daisy didn't meet my eyes again, helping herself to another sugar cube which she popped directly in her mouth instead of her tea. "You might not remember her. She was Dad's second wife's daughter."

Oh, right, Daisy's stepsister. I thought back, tried to recall. Realized I'd never actually met her. "She moved away with your stepmom when your father divorced her, right?" We were, what, fifteen? I think the marriage lasted all of six months. Daisy hadn't been in class much, I remembered that. And Rose was five years younger, went to a different school altogether.

Come to think of it, Daisy only mentioned her occasionally. I forgot all about her in my own exodus from Reading and hadn't heard anything about her in years. Not that Daisy needed to know that right now. "Is she okay?" I should have known better than to wonder where Daisy was all day. No way she'd have missed out on Mom's taping unless it was important. Any blame I felt slipped away into shame I'd doubted her at all. Dad, on the other hand… which made me think about Malcolm and Siobhan Doyle and Crew's question about what my father was up to.

I had to talk to Dad.

Daisy smiled in that brittle way that told me she was hiding something from me. "She'll be fine," she said. "Should I go see your mom tonight, do you think?"

I shook my head, letting her have her privacy. If Daisy needed me to know, needed my help, she'd tell me. Or I'd pry it out of her eventually. For now, if focusing on Mom was beneficial, then so be it.

"Just leave her for the night," I said. "But I'm worried about her, Day."

She nodded, beautiful face tight with worry. "She wants so much to make this work," she said. "You know how hard she is on herself, Fee."

Actually, I didn't. "She is?" Well, I knew she was with this baking thing. Sort of. From what I figured out.

Daisy went on like she assumed I understood what she understood. "She's been so frustrated since she retired. Feeling useless. I know it has to be hard for her." She what? Since when? "When your father retired, well, she thought that would solve everything. But the two of them have been getting on each other's last nerve." She eye-rolled again, laughed a little. How was it I knew nothing of this, and my bestie knew everything? That faint resentment I'd felt in the fall about Mom confiding in Daisy resurfaced while she went on, oblivious. "Working for you, helping out here? I think it's been great for both of them." I'd been lucky to have them, that was for sure, and taking on the annex was possible, in part, knowing they'd be there to help me if I needed it. "But your mother wants this for herself. We all want something that's ours. Especially now that John—" Daisy shut up so fast I watched horror cross her face before she carefully schooled her expression to pleasant pretend nothing happened, nothing to see here, carry on my wayward daughter.

Hell no, to the *nuh-uh.*

She had to know I was going to ask questions. Had to. And took a blurty page from my book. "So, his wife wanted a divorce?" Took me a second to realize she wasn't talking about Mom and Dad, a shock of terror washing over me until I understood the distraction was leading back to the murder. Daisy must have overheard the conversation I'd been having with Bonnie.

I'd give her one thing, her distraction technique, while needing work, did wonders for my heart health. I felt like I'd run about ten miles at top speed the way it pounded in my chest in reaction to my fear for my mother and father.

"Supposedly Joyce was having an affair with him last year," I said. "And the winner from last season, too." I thought about Janet and Mom's mention of her history with possible sabotage of other contestants. She'd been in Mom's kitchen with Vivian. Had she done the deed? Or showed Vivian what to do?

"Sounds like at least two women in his life wanted him dead," Daisy said, "and they're both under one roof."

That could get messy.

"How about the others?" Daisy sipped her tea, all innocence. I could have prodded her further about my parents, wanted to. But my traitor brain wound around the mystery of Ron Williams's murder and shunted me sideways away from the more brutal and terrifying possibility my parents weren't okay. And that I was the last to know. Wasn't going there. Not tonight.

"Janet," I ticked the woman's name off on my index finger. "Molly, though according to Bonnie she wasn't having an affair with Ron." Smart girl. "That leaves Clara." The show creator could have had a history with him. "Olivia was there. Vivian."

Daisy sighed over her cup. "As much as we'd both like to accuse Vivian, it's likely this has nothing to do with her."

"Not even Mom?" I shrugged that off. "Fine, okay. But according to Mom, Janet has a history of doing nasty things to get what she wants. At least to other contestants."

"Were she and Ron still an item?" Daisy waggled her eyebrows at me. "Getting dumped is as good a reason for murder as any."

True enough. "I don't know," I said. "But that does make sense." So hard to care when Mom's sad face resurfaced in my mind. "Day, for the first time? I don't feel compelled to snoop. Mom's more important."

She set her cup aside, gray eyes hurting for me, for Mom. While I almost reopened the question about her sudden trip to the capital. Rose. Did I have to worry about Daisy, too?

Instead, she stood, hugged me. Got her coat and quietly left. I stared glumly into my teacup as Daisy said good night, leaving me to ponder murder, my parents and the always frustrating Crew Turner. Who, it seemed, wouldn't be coming to visit tomorrow night. Not unless he was planning to arrest me. Right now? That might be the best option I had open to anything resembling a date with him. Some people liked handcuffs, right?

Bummed out but too tired to let it own me, I retreated to my apartment where I contemplated the white card with the block letters spelling Siobhan Doyle's name well into the night.

CHAPTER SIXTEEN

I exited Alicia's office, shaking Jared's hand before accepting the parting squeeze his girlfriend offered me.

"Thanks, guys," I said, pausing to slip on my coat as the morning rush of guests passed through the lobby of the Lodge. "Progress looks amazing on the annex."

Alicia beamed at me, hands clasped together under her chin while Jared's lopsided smile reminded me of how young they both were. Not that I didn't trust them. I did, implicitly. But they still had that shiny surface to them despite the less than savory dealings Jared's father, Pete, had dragged them into. Dealing with the elder Wilkins's fraud could have left his son bitter and angry. I think Alicia was exactly who he needed at his side. Even she had her history with Jared's father, served her time as his old assistant before he died. And her still missing brother, the young drug dealer, Pitch, had to weigh on her heart. But such hardships hadn't touched the two of them further than to scrape a bit off the surface. I was grateful they retained their cheerful optimism.

Gave me hope mine might show up someday and take up residence again.

"You didn't have to come all the way up here for this meeting," Alicia said, guiding me out into the lobby. "We could have come to Petunia's."

Jared winked at me, glanced at the entry to the dining room. "I don't think this meeting was really on Fee's mind," he said.

Her eyes flew wide, and she grinned. "You're terrible," she breathed at me. "You're going to give poor Crew a heart attack one of these days."

Nice to know from their expressions they didn't judge me for snooping. And yes, they were right. I could have had them come to Petunia's for a coffee and a chat there. But this was the perfect excuse to get my butt near the set again, a long night of thinking and grumbling to myself over the mystery ending in a change of venue for our get-together.

"Someone has to solve crimes around here," Jared said, lighthearted enough I knew he was teasing, but with the kind of focus that told me he also believed what he said. "Go get 'em, Fee." He nodded toward the staff hallway leading past the bathrooms. "I hear the back entry might be open."

I beamed a smile at him before hurrying/not hurrying toward the washroom sign, slipping past the gathering of skiers heading out for the day, dodging the baleful stare cast my way by my cousin, Robert. Crew made a huge mistake leaving him on guard at the main doors to the set, so easily distracted by pretty girls in ski suits that when he turned his head to smirk, thick 70's mustache twitching, beer gut a bit less prominent as he straightened up when a pair of blondes walked by, I was able to slip into the back hall without him seeing me go, grinning to myself.

Idiot. I'd get him fired one of these days. That would teach him for a) taking a job he knew I couldn't have, b) making comments about my weight and c) being alive in general. Not to mention his delight in calling me that most hated of nicknames, Fanny.

Evil firing scheme unfolding in my head, I nodded to a group of employees heading out of the staff area and waited until they passed the towering fake plants by the bathrooms before trying the side door to the dining room. Jared hadn't misled me, the handle turning easily. I slipped inside, closing it behind me after a quick peek to be sure no one would see me enter.

Voices echoed toward me from the main set, carrying over the fake walls that made up the sound stage. I drifted toward the green room, not sure exactly what I was looking for now that I was here. I almost ran right into Dale who caught me with both hands, startled, before tugging me sideways and out of sight behind a backdrop just as two women's voices, loud all of a sudden, broke out next to us.

"You can't just pack up now." Olivia's best political tone grated on me at the best of times, but knowing how much this dumb show had hurt my mother? Not to mention a murder. Yes, Mom came first. She needed to let them just wrap up and get lost. I found myself not really caring who killed Ron Williams as Clara spoke.

"We're not," the showrunner sounded like she spoke between clenched teeth. "I just got word from the studio. We have to finish taping. We've invested too much time and money into this little side project of yours to quit now."

"Let me assure you," Olivia said, rather too gushy for my liking, "there will be no further hiccups—"

"And let me assure *you*," Clara cut her off, "old friends or not," and that sounded questionable, "owe you one or not, Olivia Walker, make no mistake I have my own career to consider way ahead of your little town." I heard the mayor splutter, but Clara was faster. "We are going to get this show done fast and furious so we can move the hell on before something else happens." The sound of footsteps echoed, voices fading while the pair strode off. I turned to Dale who looked nervous.

"They have to be kidding." I shook my head at him. "Is this not a disaster waiting to happen?"

He shrugged. "From what I know, the studio likes the controversy, figures it will increase views, at least for this episode." He looked tired, running a hand over his face. "Honestly, I think it's a mistake. They're going to have Patrice sit in as the third judge. But I think the show is on its way out, no matter what Clara wants." Dale's lips twisted into a frustrated grimace. "And long overdue. Everyone knows it."

"What about Ron's cookbook launch?" I kept my voice down as more footsteps walked past us, grateful Dale was at least willing to talk to me.

The young assistant's expression turned from nervous to bitter. "Whatever," he said. "The man can't cook to save his soul, let alone write a book about it. Hardly a newsflash, either." He cocked his head to one side, nodded. I was close enough to him I heard the voice on the other end of his headphones even through the heavy foam. "Listen, I have to go. Our new third just arrived, and I have to prep her."

I caught his hand before he could stride off. "Who?"

He leaned around the backdrop hiding us and pointed and I quickly peeked out, not really as surprised as I could have been to find Joyce Young, beaming a smile, escorted by Clara toward the main stage.

The man she had an affair with—and probably dumped her from her reaction to his death—dies and she's suddenly back on the show? Motive for murder anyone?

"Wait, does that mean Mom's segment won't air?" Relief washed through me when Dale nodded.

"They're calling this a tribute show now, using the past champion, runner-up and current leader as the contestants." He shrugged. "That's show business."

"Did you know Janet cheats?" I prodded him while Dale hesitated, eyes meeting mine full of regret.

"I should have checked your mother's set more carefully," he said. "It's common knowledge, at least at the crew level." He grimaced like he wished it were otherwise while regretting not doing something about it sooner. "I figured she'd go after Molly, Fee." Which meant he checked that set, not Mom's. "I'm so sorry."

Not his fault. Not if Clara knew.

"I really have to go." Dale pointed to a shadowy corner across the back of the set. "I should kick you out, but I'm over this job." He laughed softly. "Just stay out of sight. And trouble. And cheer for Molly, won't you?" Dale waved and left me there while I exhaled the comforting feeling that Mom wouldn't be mocked on a national level, at least.

Now to get through to her she wasn't a failure.

The corner he showed me turned out to be an even better vantage point than the one I'd occupied only yesterday. Wow, was it really yesterday? I had a clear view between the placement of a fake wall and the back of the set into the sound stage and all three kitchens.

Though it really wasn't a good idea—I could get caught at any second—I spent the next several hours on aching feet, watching Molly bake her way to success. She really was impressive, I had to admit it, better than the other two women, hands down, and better than Mom, though I only allowed that thought for a moment.

When the timers went off, the clock ticked down, each round a half-hour allotment that Clara ruthlessly enforced, Molly came out the clear winner. No more multiple takes or endless banter. The showrunner was all business today. I could only imagine she wanted this done and the set and crew out. Likely they'd be filming any extras they needed when they returned to their regular location. For now, in crisp thirty-minute rounds of confectionary deliciousness, the three women battled with sugar, flour and the kind of dizzying creative talent I could only dream of.

Round one was Molly's the instant she heated her meringue with a layer of colored sugar that tinted the tips a deep red when fired with her hand torch. Round two she won with a fluffy incarnation of chocolate and peaches, towering sugar spun over the surface in a maze of sparkling sweet lines that looked like a spider's web. I barely remembered what the other two baked. Who was I kidding? I don't recall at all. Molly's work was just head and shoulders above and beyond and I found myself rooting for her despite knowing, positive when even Vivian tasted the final effort—a pie of berries and caramel and some kind of mystery spice I'd never heard of—and smiled her delight at the result.

I was surprised to find Joyce was announced second, though from the look on her face she wasn't happy about her placement.

But Janet's reaction to coming in third? Epically disastrous, especially when all three judges criticized all of her creations on taste and, in the case of her final bake, the hardness of the end result, if not design. I'd never seen a full-grown woman throw an actual hissy fit before, though she did fall short of literally throwing her offerings at the judges.

Barely.

"This stupid show was rigged!" She spit those words right into the camera as if she hadn't skewed things in her own favor all along. She turned on Joyce, lunging for her. "You sabotaged me, you witch!"

"Like you never did to me, you lying cheat!" The runner-up wasn't backing down from her rival in the least. Janet didn't make it to claw at Joyce's eyes, though she looked like that was her ideal endgame. Was she just trying to ruin the take, perhaps? Didn't seem to matter to Clara. Instead, she called, "Cut!" just before Dale leaped in and grabbed Janet, holding her back. Someone's voice echoed with, "That's a wrap!" I realized at the same instant Janet seemed to the show was, for now, over.

Then, as if by magic, the crew began to move, striking the set while last year's star shrieked her fury at no one in particular. I was suddenly exposed, the wall in front of me folding in half and then in two as two crew moved with efficient precision, the kitchens already disappearing when more hands appeared to undo what had been done to the Lodge's dining room.

Janet's anger faded to haphazard spluttering, her face so red I was sure she'd pop a vein. Everyone ignored her, including Dale who stepped off when it was apparent Janet wasn't going to attack anyone further. Molly hugged Joyce, Olivia and Vivian going to her to shake her hand and, I could only guess, congratulate her. I caught Dale beaming a smile at me, both thumbs up and I waved back, delighted he was happy for the girl he clearly cared about. Caught sight of Crew, his blue eyes fixed on me when he called out at the top of his voice, loud enough to catch everyone's attention.

"While congratulations are in order," he nodded to Molly whose excitement faded as he went on, "this set," his vocal volume dropped while everyone turned to face him, "and everyone and everything in it," he turned to address Clara who glared at him, "are staying where they are."

"I have a show to finish," she said.

"And I have a murder to solve," he said. "Guess which one takes precedence?"

CHAPTER SEVENTEEN

I slipped out the back while Crew was distracted, not really wanting to talk to him right now anyway. He had things handled and there wasn't much else for me to do at this point. Instead, I went home, trying to be happy for Molly and figure out how to tell Mom she didn't have to worry about anyone seeing the episode without hurting her feelings her segment wasn't going to be used after all.

It was a catch-22, wasn't it? The indignity of being torn to shreds by a dead guy, to go through all that prep and hard work only to have her bit of the show axed. I didn't know how to feel about it so I was pretty sure Mom wouldn't either.

Which, of course, meant one thing. I had to talk to Daisy first. Surely, she'd know what to do about it.

As I drove down the mountain, I had to laugh at myself and my reaction the night before to Mom's attachment to Daisy, how she told her everything, it seemed, even things she didn't tell me. Because wasn't I about to do exactly the same thing? And did that mean Dad used her for a sounding board, too?

Daisy Bruce, the Fleming Whisperer. Poor dear.

I parked in the driveway, taking a moment to slip over to the annex to check on the progress Jared mentioned at our meeting earlier. Yes, I was paying attention and it had been a good chance to touch base with him and Alicia on the project. While I might have been distracted, my livelihood was pretty important to me, too.

I checked on the new flooring they'd brought in, approved it and the multi-colored layering of the hardwood—loved it, actually—grinning to myself about the excellent taste Alicia had compared to anything I would have found (while wondering about the price tag and deciding to stress over the money I was spending later). That job done, I circled the fence between the two yards and headed past the Carriage House toward the pond and the kitchen door.

Head down, mind on other things, I wasn't expecting the sound of voices. As soon as I heard talking, I ducked sideways into the bushes, then wondered what kind of person's instinctual reaction to hearing people talking was to eavesdrop even as the man's Irish accent registered.

I was suddenly grateful for my suspicious nature,

thanks. Trouble was, I couldn't hear clearly, just caught the mumbling sound of his voice, the high-pitched answer from who sounded like Bonnie Williams. I snuck a peek, caught sight of a hulking suit and, just past the giant bully boy, Malcolm Murray's face.

I was right about Bonnie. She huffed something at him I didn't catch before pushing past him and hurrying to the kitchen door, through it and into the house. Maybe I should have felt more cautious about approaching the gathering of alleged criminals in my backyard, but anger piqued, and I was in no mood for any kind of criminal anything at my doorstep.

Malcolm spotted me as I stomped toward him, his two boys flanking him in their dark suits, black leather gloves, sunglasses. The normally charming and rakishly handsome, if older, gray-haired Irish mob boss's typical friendliness was nowhere to be seen. If anything, he was colder than the January morning, colder than he'd been at the Lodge when I'd seen him yesterday.

Didn't stop me from confronting him, though the icy look in his green eyes reminded me I wasn't dealing with a friend here. He was a criminal and would more than likely cut my throat and leave me dead in a ditch if it served him.

Sobering thought.

"Can I help you with something, Malcolm?" There was a time I was afraid of him, not so long ago, in fact. Sitting in the back of his car while he handed me a card with a woman's name on it. I'd thought then he'd meant me harm, and he'd been smiling and even kind. Funny, facing him down with his inner wolf showing? Made him less scary. Go figure.

"If it were your business, I'd have said so."

Did he really just think he could get away with that in my place? I closed the distance between us so fast his boys didn't get a chance to respond. And from the flicker of grudging respect and the faintest smile that pulled on Malcolm's lips as I jabbed him in the chest with one finger, I'd impressed him. He waved off his bullies while I spoke, and I have no doubt if he hadn't, I'd be dead.

"You do your business in your house," I said. "And keep it out of mine. Or you're no longer welcome at Petunia's."

His grin appeared, no kindness in it. "Understood." He looked down at my finger, still pressed against him. I took the hint and knew my luck was at the limit, backing off ever so slightly, just enough he got the message I wasn't going to let him walk all over me. "I'm just here to collect on a debt owed an associate. No intent to disrespect you, Fiona, lass."

"Like I said," I snapped. "Your business happens in your house. Not mine." Wait a second. "Is that why you were at the Lodge yesterday? To collect on a debt? Whose?"

His eyes tightened around the edges, but he answered smoothly enough. "Ron Williams owes a colleague some money. With his death, that debt is passed on to his lovely wife." He barked a laugh while his boys echoed him. "She's a charming piece of work."

Tell me about it. And yet, it felt impossibly unlikely someone like Ron Williams was borrowing money from someone Malcolm Murry might know. Unless.

"Did he have a gambling problem?" I'd dealt with that before, though more locally when the young couple who took over the flower shop had a run-in with Malcolm. Simon Jacob had lost his wife Terri over his habit, though she kept the shop. Smart girl, bought all my flowers from her.

Malcolm shrugged, gestured to his boys who turned to go. Damn it, the side gate. I had to fix it. Would fix it. Today. Right after I solved world hunger and got my pug a pedicure.

"Fiona." Malcolm paused, then sighed as he seemed to deflate somewhat. "I know you're protecting your da, or think you are, avoiding the truth. But there's that which you need to know." He nodded to me. "Look her up. And call me when you do."

I let him go, hugging myself, wishing I'd never heard of Malcolm Murray. When I finally headed for the house, I was shivering from the cold, from standing there in the crisp wind, unwinding all the possible scenarios that I might uncover, from the most ridiculous—I was an heiress to some amazing Irish throne or something—to the horrific—Dad was a murderer, a serial killer—to the desperately heartbreaking—Dad cheated on Mom with this Siobhan woman. I was so distracted by my own fear I almost collided with Bonnie who clutched at me when I entered the kitchen door, hugging me abruptly.

"I have no idea what that horrible man wanted." She shook me a little, pushing me away while Daisy made a face over Bonnie's shoulder like she wanted to rescue me.

Instead, I seated the shaking woman and confronted her. "Ron was gambling. He borrowed money from the mob. And now he's dead and you owe what he owed."

She gaped at me like I'd grown three heads and told her aliens landed next door. But it wasn't her response that caught my attention. At that very moment, Joyce slipped into the kitchen. Stopped. Stared, and blanched. Then scurried out again.

Which told me my answers to this particular bit of the mystery had nothing to do with Bonnie.

CHAPTER EIGHTEEN

I left the shaken widow with Daisy, following Joyce upstairs and catching her before she could close her door behind her. From the guarded look in her eyes, she knew exactly why I was there, so I didn't bother to pretend I was offering fresh towels.

"You know why Ron owed money he couldn't repay," I said.

She exhaled like she'd been holding her breath, cheeks pink from either the exertion of her climb up the stairs to the second floor or just from nervousness, but she nodded in agreement and opened her door. An invitation I wasn't about to question, slipping inside and turning to face her in the quiet of the softly flowered interior of the Lavender Room.

"I didn't kill Ron." Joyce had caught the blurting disease too, apparently. Her hands flapped at me, between us, as if desperate for me to believe her sincerity just by their negating motions. "I swear, I didn't. Yes, I was upset." She turned and paced into the pale purple of the flowery suite, her feet swishing on the thick carpeting before she sank to the delicately quilted coverlet, the gauze curtain over the four-poster wafting from the motion of her descent. "I loved him once." She snuffled and I fetched another tissue, this one for the mistress instead of the wife, sitting next to her as she went on. "I was so sure he loved me, too. He told me he did, that he was going to leave that horrible woman for me." She blew her nose with a faint honking sound before sagging, shoulders rounding so far forward I was afraid she might fold in half at some point. "When Janet started to win, he dropped me like I'd caught some disease. And he was right there with her, at her side, when she cheated her way to victory." She frowned at me before patting my hand in my lap. "I feel so badly for your mother. That tart is a menace and I'm so glad Molly won today. Serves Janet right."

"Not to mention while you were second, you still got to defeat her." I accepted her little nod as agreement. "She accused you of sabotaging her like she did to you. Did you?"

Joyce's eyes narrowed. "I wish," she said. "Thing is, she's a great baker. She didn't need to cheat. But she's also a horrible person." She seemed happy to be vindicated, though. "I snuck a taste of her last bake. It was definitely off. Hard as a rock."

So, someone gave Janet a taste of her own medicine. The same person who killed Ron? "You have to admit it looks bad, Joyce." It really did, especially if Janet's baking was deliberately tampered with. That screamed revenge and no one had more to hate her for and want payback than the woman sitting in front of me. At least, that I'd uncovered so far. "The sheriff is going to want to know everything. It could really help your case if you get it all sorted out in your head. With someone who knows him." Okay, so I wasn't above pretending I might be able to cut her a deal of some kind if it got me somewhere. No need for her to know I'd likely get her deeper in trouble was there? Sure, I felt for her, but then again, she knowingly had an affair with a married man. Considering my own past and my ex-boyfriend's cheating ways? Sympathy was a bit thin in this instance.

Joyce seemed to buy my ploy, though, eagerness returning to her expression, her tears drying up as she leaned closer. "I just wanted to talk to Ron, that's all. That's the only reason I was here." She snuffled, staring down at the tissue in her hands. "There's so much security around the show's normal location and his house, too. Not to mention his wife." She made that sound like she still cared about him, and that Bonnie wasn't worth smearing her shoe over. Since I'd come to understand the victim's partner wasn't an angel herself, I guess I could let it go in favor of some answers. "I figured this location shoot offered me the best chance to see him in person. To get him alone."

"And what? Change his mind?" I almost scoffed, this close to laughing in her face. She had no idea and really needed to get some self-respect. And hadn't she met the fact he'd died with an expression of relief? I checked my surge of anger, knew it came from deep hurts and Ryan's betrayal and had nothing to do with what was going on here and now. Didn't help much, though.

At least Joyce didn't seem to notice. "Maybe," she said. "He had to have seen through Janet by now. Or dumped her in favor of the new girl." Did that mean she wasn't lying to herself? That she understood Ron's game and still pined for him? Seriously? I wanted to get up and go wash my hands or shower or something to get the greasy feeling off me. Trouble was, it wasn't on the surface, and I had no idea how to scrub my brain. Believe me, I'd tried.

"I didn't know Bonnie had come to stay here," she said. "I wouldn't have if I'd known. I swear." She sighed then, a giant gust of air escaping her, with the barest tremor at the end. Waking my empathy, damn it.

"Ron's death gave you a chance to get back on the show." That was better. Not delivered as a jab, though, just as truth.

Joyce finally reacted, her face twisting in anger before she shrugged. "Dale spotted me," she said. "Told Clara I was here. When she approached me, how could I say no? For a chance to redeem myself?"

I understood that motivation, at least. Just wished Mom had the same opportunity. And again felt myself despising this woman, this time for removing my mother's chance to show the world she was great at what she did.

If Joyce had been able to see inside my head right then? She wouldn't have said another word. Instead, she stared out the window, the faint light from the bathroom creating shadows over both of us, streetlights catching glints as snow began to fall.

"I know how your mother feels," she said. "The exact same thing happened to me that last episode. What happened to her yesterday. Janet messed with my ingredients. It was my fault, though. I didn't taste my batter." The now-familiar litany of a blaming baker. Kind of crushing she had the nerve to sound just like Mom. "Not that it would have mattered. By the time I could have, I wouldn't have been able to make a fresh batch anyway." There was that. The timelines were so tight… I wondered if telling Mom that would help?

"Janet won because she cheated. But the worst part?" She turned back, met my eyes with her own full of hurt. "No one cared. Not Ron, not Clara. No one, Fee. After a season thinking these people gave a crap about me? That hurt most of all."

"What happened that Ron chose Janet over you?" The cheating?

Joyce winced. "I gave him an ultimatum," she said. "I wanted him to commit to me." Wow, how long had they known each other? Sure, the guy cheated, but surely, she had to know a short season of TV wasn't the kind of fling that led to long-term relationships? "The next night Janet won because of him. She cheated her way to the finish line from then on without being challenged." She choked on a sob, the tissue crumpling in her fingers pressed to her lips. "I should have won the show *and* Ron."

This time I had to get up, to stride away a step and catch my breath as my stomach turned over. Sure, Bonnie was a piece of work who only held on to Ron for his money. But this woman? How despicable could you get?

"Ron ruined me," she whispered. "Janet, too."

"Bit of a stretch, isn't it?" I turned back to her, cleared my throat when she jerked in response. "It's just a cooking show, Joyce."

She started to shake, face tightening in anger as she sat there and trembled in response. "You have no idea." She shook her head, a quick, sharp gesture. "Thanks to the constant demands of the show, film timing, my public catastrophic failure in the final episode? I lost everything. My husband." Should have thought about that before she cheated, huh? "My business." Honestly, I needed to get a grip and stop being so hard on her. "My reputation." Deep breath.

"I'm sorry," I said, really meaning it. "I didn't know."

"I didn't kill Ron Williams," Joyce said, "but I meant what I said earlier. Despite still loving him, I'm glad that bastard is dead."

CHAPTER NINETEEN

Did she know she just jumped her way to #1 on my suspect list? She must have because Joyce surged to her feet and came at me with a desperate expression and a gooey tissue outstretched, both of which made me flinch.

"I know what that sounds like." She dropped her hands suddenly to her sides again, stopping her forward motion so abruptly I was breathless from not knowing if I should keep backpedaling or hold my ground. "Tell the sheriff whatever suits you. But I didn't do it."

Not much to say, except, of course, as I was about to leave, I paused with an internal take to task for forgetting the reason I came up here in the first place.

"Ron's debt?" I waited, hoping for an answer.

Disappointment wasn't my favorite emotion, but that's all I got out of her when she turned away, head down.

"I don't know specifics," she said, "but he was in financial trouble when I was with him. That was six months ago. Then, suddenly he seemed to have money again, just before he traded me in for Janet."

Interesting.

I left her then, slowly descending to the foyer, mind spinning. Knowing I needed to call Crew, wondering how that conversation would go over while hating that I hesitated. I caught sight of Daisy exiting the kitchen, headed my way, and took a leap as I hurried the rest of the way downstairs, reaching for the coat rack and my wool jacket, not pausing to go to the kitchen for my warmer one. I wasn't going far or planning to take long.

"Can you stay?" I was already out the door, waving while she nodded and smiled and waved back, mournful Petunia hovering at her heels. The pug would punish me later for leaving her behind. So be it. This trip I needed to take on my own.

It was a short walk to Crew's little house, just two streets over from Mom and Dad. Convenient, how small the interior of Reading was, how easy it could be to get around. The faint fall of fresh snow was just enough to add a tiny squeak under my boots, the air chill but still again. A perfect evening for a brisk march to my doom at the hands of Crew Turner.

Hey, I had an excuse, right? He was supposed to

come see me tonight and he hadn't. So, it was up to me to make the first move.

Sure, Fee. Keep spinning those lies if it makes you feel better about yourself.

It took a lot not to slow as I neared his front door, to push myself physically up his walkway, past the short shrubs lining his entry, up the two concrete steps and to raise my mitten and knock. Almost more than I had in me. Why was I here again? My phone from the privacy of my basement apartment seemed much more logical even as I tapped on the glass and waited.

And waited. This was dumb, he probably wasn't even home. Right, that's why there were lights on inside and his truck was parked in the driveway. Because he wasn't home. I waffled, wavering as I half turned to leave, knocking more forcefully and holding my breath while I silently berated myself for being a nervous nelly because he was just a person for goodness sakes and for coming here in the first place since, honestly, what was I hoping to achieve?

I've never felt time hold its breath the way it seemed to that long few seconds I hovered, indecision creating a whirling vortex of growing anxiety in my tummy while I thought about what my real reasons for coming to Crew's house might be. Refused to accept I just wanted to see him in his natural habitat, hoped maybe the softness I'd seen in him might come out again if we weren't in a murderous setting. There had been enough flickers of who I figured he really was over the last eighteen months I just couldn't let go of the possibility. His request to speak privately only fed my meager hopes. Hormones didn't play a part or anything, did they? Though I couldn't get past thinking, in the final breath I took as a shadow passed between the interior light and the door's glass that this could be construed as a desperate single woman's attempt to nab her a man, gosh darn it.

The door opened, Crew standing on the other side, the outer light coming on as he hit the switch. Chill air mixed with the warm exiting his front door past his wide chest and lean hips, longish dark hair still wet from the shower. The scent of him and the soap he'd used, the dampness clinging to him washed over me in an intoxicating rush of overwhelm that almost knocked me off the top step.

His eyebrows rose, startled expression turning serious as he reached out and caught me before I could stumble backward and brain myself on his shrubs.

"Fee." He smiled faintly, glanced over my shoulder, then stepped aside. He seemed surprised I was alone for some reason. "Come in."

I rushed inside before I could run away, heart pounding, finding it hard to swallow past the dryness in my now tight throat while he closed the door behind me, standing so close I could see the faint line across his cheek where he'd missed a bit of hair shaving. This was a terrible idea. I had to go before I did something stupid like grab him and throw him on the couch conveniently located just a few feet away—

Fee. Get a grip, already.

"Are you okay?" He leaned closer, concern clear while I backed away from him two steps, bumping gracefully into the small table he kept his keys and wallet on, sending them both tumbling to the tile floor. I spent the next thirty or so seconds stumbling through an apology jacked with stuttering and incoherency while he reassured me and righted the table, smiling when he was done. He straightened, holding out one hand, the other in his back pocket. "Can I take your coat?"

"I'm not staying." I had to just throw that at him like he'd offended me, right? Crew's smile faded but he nodded, hand falling to his side. "Daisy. I left her. At Petunia's. With Petunia." Oh my god. There was something seriously wrong with me.

Crew seemed to understand. "Did you need something?"

Boy, did I. About a half-hour of sexy time—

"I have information for you." Saved by the happy crushing truth of my snooping.

Instead of reacting like he seemed accustomed to these days, Crew just nodded. "Did you want a beer?" He headed for the kitchen, leaving me at the entry of his small house while he crossed the tile on bare feet, a fire crackling in the hearth on the far side of the room, the smell of something resembling spaghetti sauce in the air. I'd interrupted his dinner, obviously, but when I turned to go, to just let the poor guy have time to unwind because this really had gone from a terrible idea to dismally pathetic, he cracked a bottle open and held it out to me.

Traitor feet. They kicked off my boots before I could stop them and carried me to the threshold of his kitchen, hand rising to take the chilled glass, condensation forming on the dark surface. He opened a second, leaning across the counter with his elbows on the surface, looking up at me while he sipped and waited.

I don't know what freaked me out more, his calm, unjudging attitude or the fact I was standing in his house having a beer and wondering what a date would feel like. Like this?

The next several minutes felt surreal. The drink went down so fast I barely tasted it, grateful for the lubrication of my dry throat as I told him about Malcolm, Bonnie and Joyce. Crew opened another beer for me, then one for himself, the fridge humming softly to life when he closed the door again. He paused to stir a pot of sauce on the stove, nodding while I wrapped up my last conversation with Joyce, my suspicions and her confirmation Janet had been sabotaged herself, turning a knob down as he let the tomato-based deliciousness simmer.

"Can I ask you something?" His deep voice held none of the usual condemnation or disappointment or anger that it typically did in times like this. Just pure curiosity. Couldn't he at least pretend he was mad at me so I could maintain the status quo and not shiver inside my wool coat, wondering what was going on here and what changed? He took my silence for agreement because he asked anyway. "Why do you bring what you learn to me? Why not just go to your dad? You know what I'm going to say. So why?"

I gaped, fingers spasming on my beer.

Crew went on like he didn't know my brain was imploding. "You already know what I'm going to do, there's more than enough precedence set. I'm going to yell at you for interfering or tell you to mind your own business or treat you like you're a pain in my ass and you still bring me what I need to solve cases. You never, ever quit." His blue eyes met mine then, softer than they'd ever seemed, not a trace of anger in him. Wait, was that respect? Hello, really? "Why, Fee? Why haven't you given up on me?"

Given up on… stutter, splutter, choke. "I don't go looking," I said. Blushed. "Mostly. I swear, this stuff falls in my lap."

He waved that off. Fell still, waiting.

Did I have an answer for him? I guess I did, tied to the new fear I only now realized Dad's comment had woken in me. That somehow Crew's job was in danger, and it was my fault. "I want to help," I said. "Help you. And I'm good at it. You're good at it. And I trust you." There. Said it.

Crew nodded slowly, sipped his beer. "I assumed you've been screwing with me, and I'm sorry for that." He stared at the bottle, not speaking before he rushed on. "Now I get you had no idea. You weren't setting me up. Or mocking me, pushing me. You had no clue how much pressure I've been getting. From

Olivia and the council. About your dad and you." I shook my head, feeling misery rise. I'd had an inkling of it in October, but no details. "It's actually made me want to quit, Fee. I've never quit anything in my life, but having John and Fiona Fleming shoved in my face over and over again? That's brought me about as close as anything ever has." He sighed deeply, standing straighter, shrugging with a faint smile. "And you know what? When I thought you did know, it wasn't so bad. I could almost put up with it. Until I found out you didn't. That you were totally oblivious. You were making my life miserable, and you didn't know you were doing it. Aside from the obvious."

I needed to go. This was too much. Was he quitting? Leaving Reading because of me and Dad? That was the last thing I wanted.

"I understand, though." Crew bobbed a nod, almost to himself. "I get that it's hard for everyone to let go. John was sheriff for a lot of years. This is a small town and outsiders aren't always welcome. And with you, the golden Fleming daughter, home again when everyone thought you were long gone," wait, the what now? "I guess I was feeling a bit on the jealous side." He laughed then, downed his beer, reached into the fridge for another. Stopped. Met my eyes again.

"You're a natural, Fee. If I'd known you when you were a kid, if you'd told me you wanted to be a cop and your father said no? I'd have stood up to him for you and told him where he could shove his idea he could tell you what to do."

I didn't know if I should hug him or cry, still caught up in the golden daughter statement. Where was he getting the idea anyone wanted me home aside from Mom and Dad?

"I'm sorry," I said, choked on it. "I'll stop, I swear. Just don't quit." I set my bottle down, the base rattling on the counter. "You're great at what you do, Crew. And I'm a nosy busybody who really should just go home." I'd expected pushback, planned for a fight. This was something else entirely. If he wanted to win, he'd found a way to do it. Only it didn't feel like he was playing me. Was this the private talk he wanted to have? If so, I'd misread him about as much as he misread me. I was an idiot. He wasn't into me. That whole moment of maybe died before it could live. Whatever opportunity there had been, that day in the garden last April? I'd clung to it for no reason. And that realization sucked more than anything.

"Fee." Crew circled the counter while I turned and headed for the door. I had to get out of here before I cried or something equally stupid. He caught me before I could get those damned boots back on, but he didn't say anything while I jammed them on my feet, one heel sticking so I stumbled over the compressed leather. Getaways should have been easier than this.

And then I was blurting because I couldn't stop the words that tumbled out of my mouth. "I just, this stuff happens to me, and it doesn't seem right not to tell you because I thought I could help and now I know I'm not helping I'm really making a huge mess of everything and I'm sorry, Crew, I'm sorry." I gasped a breath, shaking my head, wishing I hadn't come here tonight.

Wishing the world would crack open and swallow me so I didn't have to meet his eyes, feel shame about making his life so hard and my own a pining waste of both our time.

When his warm hands cupped my hot cheeks, they felt chilled in comparison. A detail that went away the instant his lips covered my mouth.

CHAPTER TWENTY

So, if someone had told me that this day would end with Crew Turner kissing me, I'd probably have laughed in their face then gone home and ate an entire pint of ice cream while doing my best not to cry in my pillow. I'd imagined what it would be like, what those amazing lips would feel like pressed on mine, how his body might mold against me, how he would taste if I ever got the chance to kiss him.

Imagination? Pfft. Pale comparison.

Maybe my inner feminist should have protested the unagreed to kiss now being deployed against my lips that moved in time with his though I didn't give them the go-ahead to do so. Instead, I leaned into him, feeling my entire body sigh in answer to his touch, the delicious taste and scent and warmth of him spreading a happy ball of delighted tingling from the center of me to every extremity until I vibrated with the zinging joy that was kissing Crew Turner.

When he leaned away, I barely suppressed the soft moan of regret, thinking, rather oddly, of that same sound Petunia often used to express her own disappointment when she didn't get what she wanted. Which made me giggle ever so slightly.

Crew laughed. Threw back that handsome head of his with his dark hair curling over his collar and laughed a belly laugh that sounded like heaven.

"I don't know if I should be offended or not you're amused that I kissed you," he said, grinning down at me while I smiled breathlessly back.

"Definitely a giddy compliment," I said, not even trying to explain the pug connection and giving myself kudos for avoiding being a weirdo for once. Awesome. No, really. Awe. Some.

Crew lowered his big hands from my face, sliding them around my shoulders until he pressed me against his chest, my coat compressing under his grasp. I had trouble focusing on his eyes, though whether from the close proximity or the *close proximity* (you get what I mean, right?) I wasn't in a position to decide.

"Thanks for the info," he said, deep voice now rumbling and catching a bit. His pupils had dilated all over again, but this time for reasons that made me want to take my coat off and stay awhile after all. Daisy wouldn't mind. Especially if I told her why I didn't come home tonight.

Growl. Down, girl.

"You're welcome." I sighed into his chest and did the right thing. "You won't quit?"

He shook his head. "You're stuck with me a while," he said.

I'd take it. And leave it. "I guess I should go."

He didn't say anything for a long time. Make no mistake whatsoever. If Crew had decided me leaving wasn't what he wanted, I can promise you right here and now I would have been staying put. But he was a good boy, wasn't he? Maybe his wife's memory still lingered. There was enough in his expression, in the way he smiled at me, how his hand slid over my back a moment that told me there was a very good chance I'd be getting a date after all.

Imagine that.

He held the door for me while I slipped out, hopping to fix my boot while he shook his head and laughed again, waving when I smiled in turn.

"Stay safe out there," he said.

I felt a bit giddy as I made it all the way down his walk—without tripping and falling on my face! Yay me!—and turned to find he was still at the door, watching me. I wanted to laugh, to yell and run like a teenager who'd had her first kiss. Instead, I bobbed a ridiculous curtsy when he waved one last time, the sound of his laughter carrying as he finally closed the door.

I stood there in the street, taking a deep breath of the cool night air before pulling out my cell phone and texting Daisy I was on my way. Realized I didn't want to go home just yet the exact moment a black car with tinted windows rolled past.

I should have gone home. But I was still on a high from Crew and now that I felt about as free and clear and a bit wild as I ever had, it was time to confront the Irishman who thought he could jerk my chain and get away with it.

I stomped down the street to the stop sign where his car had pulled up, but instead of waiting, his driver peeled away in the direction of The Orange. I scowled after them and made a terrible life choice, my favorite.

Another quick text to Daisy and I found myself bouncing the five blocks to the other side of town and a confrontation with destiny. Okay, not so much, but everything just felt epic and saga-like, as if I'd walked into a Hollywood movie, the heroine with a passionate kiss for her true love off to do battle and all that. Though calling Crew my true love was a stretch. And I wasn't that much of an action hero as I shivered in my coat and wished I'd taken my car two blocks before I reached my destination.

Heroines didn't whine about the cold. *Didn't.*

Malcolm was just getting out of his car when I crossed to the front door, pausing to raise an eyebrow at me, his personal coldness still firmly in place. He could rival the bitter wind now rising against my back. Crap, that meant a chilly walk home.

"You're here," he said, voice crackling with disdain, "to ask me if I killed the sod I went to collect money from. Because you didn't get enough of me earlier, I take it. And you're as much a nosy brat as they say you are."

That was nasty and uncalled for. I scowled at him, unwilling to let him take the edge off my buzz. "And you're pissed at me for not being courageous enough to look into my father's past because I'm afraid I'm going to find something that breaks my heart."

I watched his face thaw ever so slightly, his body twitch in response.

"Am I right?" His gray eyes clouded over. "Are you a coward, lass?"

"You tell me," I said. "You're happy judging me. That's on you, Malcolm. But doesn't answer the question. You're right about that much."

He grinned at last, quick and sharp. "The man was indebted to another, for dabbling with ponies and some troubles with the taxman." The IRS? That was a new development, though hardly surprising. Someone like Ron Williams would try to defraud the government. "Not me personally. It's damned hard to collect on what's owed when he's gone and died, now, isn't it?"

I believed him. I wasn't there to ask him about Ron anyway and I think we both knew it.

"Tell me one thing," I said as he turned to enter his bar, his bullies hulking near the door.

"Aye," Malcolm said. "One thing."

"Am I going to hate my father when I'm done talking to Siobhan Doyle?" I squared myself, prepped for the answer. "Either way, I can take it. But I need to know."

Malcolm's face twisted, his gaze dropping to the sidewalk between us. He seemed like he wanted to say something, lips working, lean face tight. He finally just shook his head and turned his back on me.

"Come see me when you have that answer," he said, the door closing behind him and his bullies while I glared after him.

He could have at least gotten one of his boys to drive me home.

CHAPTER TWENTY-ONE

It was closer to go to Mom and Dad's, so I stopped in on the pretense I wanted to know how Mom was doing. The truth? I was an icicle by the time I reached their street, so it was a no-brainer to run up their walk and knock before dashing inside. Why, oh why did I leave my puffy coat in the kitchen and take my dressier wool one instead?

My need for warmth came up against a giant roadblock. The front door was locked tight and though there were lights on, Mom's car and Dad's truck were gone. How could they both be out at a time like this? I stood on the stoop, shivering from the horrible wind I'd been forced to walk into all this way, stomping my boots to try to get some feeling in my toes while I blew into the cuffs of my mittens, fingers curling into my palms inside the soft fleece in a desperate attempt to conserve heat. It took me a long moment to admit defeat and head back into the wind, winding my scarf a little more firmly around my lower face and gritting my teeth against the chill.

Most of the shine that I'd gained from Crew's kiss had worn off by the time I hurried through the front door of Petunia's, shivering so violently I was positive I'd never be warm again. Daisy rushed to my side, tugging me into the kitchen, Petunia waddling after us. My bestie, bless her heart, stripped my boots from my freezing feet, my mittens from my clawed hands and tucked warm towels around both sets of extremities before brewing me a hot pot of tea.

By the time I could talk past my chattering teeth, toes and fingers on fire with the tingling return of warmth, she brushed off my apology for taking so long.

"Fee," she said, turning toward the window behind her, an anxious look on her face before she spun back to me. "I'm worried about your mother."

Wait, Mom was here? No, not here. I could see it now, the lights over the fence. Someone was in the annex. Cold forgotten, I bundled back up, leaving Daisy with Petunia and heading out into the freezing night with my puffy coat protecting me this time. It was after 9PM, what was Mom doing here? I shuddered at the return of winter's touch but ran the distance to the fence and around the Carriage House before hurrying up the back path to the kitchen door and bustling inside.

To find my mother sitting alone in the work lights, the mostly completed kitchen huge compared to her despite her down jacket and adorable fur hat with the matching mittens in her lap. I went to her, sat next to her, took her hand in mine. She clutched at me, bringing my cold fingers to her mouth, and blowing on them like she used to when I was a little girl. And then she cried, and I cried with her, finally getting the Mom hug and giving the daughter one I'd wanted to yesterday.

When we both finished, faster than I expected, I sat back and accepted the tissue from her pocket. That was my mom, always prepared. I dabbed at my tears, blew my nose while she did the same. She seemed calmer, but still not quite herself. A fact she reinforced for me when she spoke.

"I never expected things to go so badly." She laughed a little, shook her head, the flaps on her hat bouncing. "Fee, I was such a fool to ever think I could compete."

"No," I said, squeezing her hand. "You did everything right. It's not your fault." I thought about what Joyce said. "Even if you had tested the batter, there was no time to change it."

"It's all right, honey," she said. "Your old mom had her butt handed to her and now I have to figure out what that means."

"It doesn't mean anything when someone cheats you out of a chance to show what you can do." I had to get through to her because I wasn't liking how this was sounding.

"I've taken on so many things in my life," Mom said, blinking and smiling at me, looking so vulnerable I wanted to hug her again, so I did. The rest of her words came out muffled from the collar of my coat. "And I've been very successful. I guess I wasn't expecting to fail quite so spectacularly and publically."

I pushed her back, jaw tight, ready to shake sense into her if I had to. "Stop that."

She touched my cheek with trembling fingers. "What does it feel like, Fee? To never doubt yourself?" Like I'd know. "You and your father, you're both so… it's effortless for you. The rest of us mere mortals have to work for it. But you and John, you have the kind of courage I wish was catching."

She did not just say that to me. "Lucille Marigold Fleming," I said, "you listen to me. I am the biggest self-doubter you've met in your entire life, and you know it. I've spent my whole adulthood wondering what the hell I did wrong and flailing from one disaster to another." Felt kind of cathartic to admit it out loud, to not have to be strong and powerful and pretend I was all put together, especially with my mother. "So, don't hand me that crap. I'm a walking danger zone." I rolled my eyes. "Murder magnet, busybody, you name it."

Her smile didn't change, softness in her eyes, tremble to her lower lip. "But you keep going," she said. "You never quit."

"I get that from you," I said. "You taught me that."

"You get that from John," she said, sighing and looking down. "Fee, you weren't here. You don't understand."

I was here. I sat across from her the whole time she—

Wait. She wasn't talking about the show.

"I wasn't," I said. "I left." I left her. I left my mom. And something happened. Did this have to do with Siobhan Doyle? Was I going to have to murder my father and hide the body? "So, tell me."

She waved off my concern. "Nothing big happened," she said while I exhaled mentally, though the tightness in my stomach didn't release. I had to research that woman and get this anxiety out of me. "I just… stopped wanting to teach. To be a principal. I felt like I was failing, Fee. And your father, he was still going strong. But when the chance came up to step away…"

"You retired." I focused on her, trying to be there for her now like I wasn't years ago, overcompensating maybe a bit but refusing to let her down. "And?" I could guess. "All of a sudden your purpose was gone." I knew that feeling, had it when Ryan cheated, and I left him and was stranded in New York those miserable few weeks before Grandmother Iris died and left me Petunia's. As terrible as her loss was, it meant a new start for me. A blessing after dealing with the judgment of most of our friends, how the few who stood by me picked sides. But the worst part was not having him in my life anymore. Not him specifically, but the familiar was gone.

Maybe not the same thing. But I could relate.

Mom's face crumpled before she pulled herself together. I wished she'd just cry it out. Instead, she sniffed and spoke. "I tried so many things. Volunteering for the council, taking on small projects. I even tried to learn to knit." She snorted a laugh and I joined her though unsure what was funny about knitting. "I just kept coming back to baking, Fee." Her eyes finally lit up. "I've always loved it. I worked at Vivian's grandparent's bakery when I was a teenager, did you know that?" I hadn't. "Walter French gave me my first job and I learned so much from him." We needed to have these talks more often. I wanted to know everything about her past. Hopefully not when so many tears and this much hurt was involved. "I should never have pushed John to retire." Again with the face scrunching as she fought tears. "It was so unfair of me. I just hated not having a job to do and he was still so wrapped up in work."

"I know he understood that, Mom," I said.

She shrugged, looked away. "Baking for Petunia's, helping you with the guests, Fee it's brought back so much to my life. I can't tell you how much I've loved it." She did smile again, at least, so I didn't have to shake her yet. "And when Daisy had me make a few silly cakes for her, well, I got cocky." She brushed off my protest before I spoke it out loud. "You don't have to comfort me. I'm well aware of the fact I took on more than I could handle. This wedding?

Seriously." Oh, crap. Please, don't tell me she was backing out? "While I'm not a fan of Vivian on the best of days, she's right. I need to leave such an important event to the professionals."

So that was what she said to Mom two months ago in the privacy of my kitchen. After breaking into my place and being a bitch to my mother. I'd yelled at Vivian in the back of her bakery while the two of us had a screaming match but without any kind of real satisfaction coming from it. Looked like she'd done the damage she'd set out to do, though, hadn't she?

"She offered me a job." Mom didn't sound excited.

I spluttered a second. "The hell she did."

Mom nodded. "Offered to apprentice me under some of her cake decorators. So I could see how the pros did it."

My head was about two seconds from exploding. Right before I hunted down Vivian and tossed her over the side of the mountain.

Violence, Fee. *So* unbecoming.

"Mom," I said, barely keeping it together but doing it because she needed me to, "you listen to me right now. Right. Now." I punctuate those two words with little shakes, finally getting to that point. Mom looked up at me from under her lashes, waiting but I'm not so sure willing to hear me. "You can bake circles around those store-bought, common, bland and dry bakery buffoons and we both know it. She's so damned jealous of Lucy Fleming and her awesomeness she will do anything—anything, Mom—to make you feel like you're beneath her." Mom didn't argue and she seemed to perk just a bit, so I went on, hoping I'd get through to her. "This has nothing to do with how awesome you are and everything to do with her ego. She would just love to get you under her thumb and crush your heart. No way we're letting that happen. No way, Mom."

I thought for a moment I had her, felt her trembling ease, her shoulders going back a bit, chin tilting upward. Until she sighed and looked away again, hands tugging free from mine.

"I've never been so embarrassed," she said. "I humiliated myself, let that man turn me into a laughingstock in front of everyone. I crumbled, Fee. I never thought I was that person. But I am. I'm the one who falls apart when tough times roll around. How can I ever trust myself again?" She spun on me then, angry, but with herself. "How can I trust my skills when a ridiculous man shouting at me makes me cry like a child in front of everyone?" She stood up, cramming her hands into her mittens, fumbling for her coat zipper, the wrong order of steps making her tsk in frustration as the fluffy ends couldn't grasp the metal tab. "This whole baking as a business thing was a terrible idea. So was working for you at all. I should go back to learning to knit or maybe teach on the internet or something that I'm good at." She hesitated while my mind spun with something to say, some way to stop her from leaving me like this. "I'm sorry, Fee. I got you into this mess. But you're going to have to hire someone to run this restaurant. And to do the wedding. I'm done."

I sat there, stunned and cold from more than the chilly temperatures, unable to think of a thing to do or say to stop Mom as she fled.

CHAPTER TWENTY-TWO

Daisy was waiting for me in the kitchen when I came back, looking sad enough I knew she already guessed what I'd encountered at the annex.

"You knew she was going to quit." I tossed my jacket to the counter, frustrated and tired and angry for Mom while Daisy looked away.

"I had a feeling," she said. "She's so hurt, Fee. I've never seen your mother like this. Not when she retired, not ever."

I sank to a stool, hard pit of unhappiness in my stomach, realizing how much I'd missed out on when it came to Mom. "You were here for her all this time," I said. Not bothering to add the caveat that I wasn't, because it wasn't necessary.

Daisy shook her head then, dark blonde hair a

halo around her face while she reached for my hand and squeezed it. "It's not like that," she said rather sharply, as if knowing where my head was, "and you can stop blaming yourself for missing out right now, young lady." Okay, so she did know what I was thinking. "Your mother was so proud of you for standing on your own, for leaving like you did. I don't think you knew just how much she wanted you to go, to find a life away from Reading."

"I'm back, though," I said. "What does that make me?"

Daisy sighed, more serious than I'd ever known her to be, as if all her bubbly delightful vivaciousness had been smothered by the darkness outside, that now lingered in the kitchen.

"She'll be okay," my best friend said, not answering my question but maybe offering something better in her reply. "And so will you."

I hugged her, too, as I had my mom, so grateful she sat there with me, that she cared enough to be here for me. When I let her go, I rubbed my face with both hands at the exact moment Petunia let a massive fart rip. It was so loud it woke her up from a nap, eliciting a yip of startled surprise while the horrifying stench that followed shifted our laughter to groans and hand waving to dispel the smell.

Nice way to end our talk.

Daisy headed home shortly thereafter. A quick check told me both Bonnie and Joyce were securely in their rooms, lights on, TV's chattering. I retreated back downstairs without disturbing either of them. It wasn't until I locked the front door and turned to go down to my apartment, I remembered I'd failed to dish the happy part of my evening to Daisy. Despite my sadness over Mom and worry about her and her state of mind, my own guilt for not being here for her the way I should have been—going to change that, you betcha—my traitor mind drifted to Crew and his lips and the way his hands felt on my skin until I crawled into bed with the fragrant pug at my side, staring at the ceiling with a well of giggles fighting to escape as naughty thoughts won over sad ones.

It was silly to linger over that kiss. More than likely he'd been just trying to shut me up, right? But the more I tried to explain away the closeness I now felt, the way he'd laughed like he really meant it, the further down the rabbit hole of holy crap maybe he does actually like me I fell. Smart or not, I could use the good feelings and tumbled into sleep to the memory of his voice.

I was still smiling the next morning when I got up and couldn't wipe the expression from my face as I showered, make coffee, ate a quick bite then got on with my routine. It wasn't until Daisy arrived, I sobered somewhat, almost resentful she shattered my mood by storming into the foyer with her purse swinging, slamming the front door behind her.

"Your mother," she said at a very unDaisylike almost shout, "is more stubborn than you are!"

"You're really surprised?" I fought to hold onto my happy and snuggled the memory of the kiss deep in my heart for further examination later. Because there would be further examination, and hopefully more memories to add to it if I had anything to say about it. "Don't tell me you tried to talk to Mom."

She eye-rolled and sighed so dramatically I laughed, not sure why it made me feel lighthearted and blaming Crew for the easing of my worry.

"Seriously," Daisy said, then grinned. "But don't you fret. I'll wear her down. You leave Lucy Fleming to me."

While I had no intention of doing so ever again, taking responsibility for my relationship with my mother now a priority, I nodded and followed her into the kitchen, listening to her rattle on about prepping breakfast since Mom wasn't coming.

It was supposed to be my mother's morning and the Jones sisters weren't working since I hadn't called them. That meant the morning meal was up to Daisy and me. Yes, I could have phoned Betty and asked her to come, but she'd slowed down so much since her first knee operation, she and Mary both seemed ready to ease themselves out of my employ. Especially when I told them about the annex purchase.

Staff. Right. I needed to hire staff.

The next hour or so was a whirlwind of Daisy bossing me around while, aproned and enthusiastic, she took over the spatula and the stove and commanded the kitchen like a wartime general. I kept meaning to tell her about Crew, but she was having so much fun I decided to wait, not wanting to interrupt her ambitious plan for French toast and some kind of croissant creation I wasn't sure she could pull off but came out surprisingly tasty in the end.

Which relegated me to serving status, not that I minded. I'd been a barista and a waiter for enough years in New York that schlepping food wasn't something I turned my nose up at. While we only had two guests, Daisy's overabundance of cooking meant I'd get a real breakfast, too, so I wasn't complaining. Neither was my pug who was a good girl in the fact she sat in the bed Mom insisted she use on the other side of the counter and waited with drool dripping from her jaws for Daisy to share the spoils. Poor thing would have to do with fruit, not that she cared. To Petunia, food was food.

The sun beamed into the kitchen, the crisp cold outside brilliant white, more snowfall making everything in the back garden glow in the brightness. It was hard not to feel happy, so I didn't fight it, singing along with Daisy as she cranked the radio, shuffling out plates and fresh bread and the full coffee carafe on dancing feet.

I paused outside the dining room door at the sound of voices, stopping myself in time when I realized the owners shouldn't be on speaking terms.

"Of course, if we decide to go ahead, it will be a contract hire, but I'm sure we can work out the details." That was Bonnie, the clink of something metal on porcelain likely a spoon and teacup.

"Did you already make this offer to Molly?"

Joyce's response didn't sound angry or upset, more curious and definitely lacking in antagonism. Interesting.

"I haven't," Bonnie said. "It's likely she'll have her own endorsements to deal with if she wins this season. Your comeback in the special tied to the controversy around Janet's cheating could give us the exposure we need to promote the book."

Well now. I got moving again, smiling as I carried a basket of fluffy pastries fresh from the oven down the right side of the room, setting it on the buffet table while smiling at the ladies. They shared a table of their own, sitting close together, Joyce returning my expression while Bonnie waved with her spoon.

"Fee, dear, the food smells delightful." She gestured at the table. "Your mother?"

I shook my head, wishing it had been. "So, the cookbook promotion is going ahead then?"

Joyce flushed a bit but seemed happy while Bonnie shrugged.

"We're in negotiations," she said.

"Nice to see you two have come to an agreement." And weird, in my opinion.

This time Joyce's discomfort was clear on her face, but Bonnie waved it off like it was yesterday's dirty news.

"There's no place for grudges when business is involved," she said. Wow, was she really that arrogant? I'd met her husband, so I guess his brand of awful came naturally to her, too. At least she sounded sober. Made me wonder if her drinking jag the day Ron died was in response to a specific stressor or a more regular occurrence. "And I need a strong launch for the book to ensure we make the lists."

"I'm still thinking about it," Joyce said then, before gushing as she went on. "It's a great opportunity and to get my hands on Ron's recipes?" She clasped her hands in front of her while I groaned internally at the terrible wording—or maybe it was just my interpretation that made it sound oddly suggestive—though Bonnie didn't seem to care. "I can't wait to test them."

They clearly didn't realize this partnership thing coming from what felt like left field gave both of them the appearance of guilt. They could have been working together long before now. And the whole animosity from Bonnie for a man she didn't love against the woman he cheated with seemed flimsy in light of this conversation.

"What makes his creations so outstanding?" Bonnie frowned at my curiosity, but Joyce didn't have her reticence. And missed the annoyed glance her new partner shot at her when she spoke, voice bubbling excitement.

"The ideas, they're old school, but with new combinations I've never heard before. Like someone took your grandmother's old-world recipes and turned them into masterpieces anyone can create." Joyce glanced at Bonnie and only then seemed to notice she'd spoken out of turn. "At least, that's what I've been told."

"You haven't seen the book yet?" I glanced at Bonnie.

"The manuscript is a carefully guarded secret for now," she sniffed at me. "Only the publisher has the final copy."

"Seems odd that Ron was able to write a book, considering I hear the filming schedule was so grueling." That's what Joyce said, didn't she? Then again, maybe he'd been working on it for a while now?

"Ronald's brilliance was undefinable," Bonnie said. "Honestly, I have no idea where he found the time. But he did, in a burst of creativity." Did he, now? "I wasn't about to question the opportunity to market him so widely."

Right, money talked.

"Now," she said like I was her servant—which, in fairness, I kind of was at the moment—"fetch me some of that delicious smelling breakfast, won't you, Fiona, dear? Joyce and I have more business to discuss."

I took the hint and my leave without telling her where she could shove her new, self-congratulatory attitude.

CHAPTER TWENTY-THREE

Daisy paused in her cooking, likely thanks to the look on my face. Something I could only guess sat in between annoyed as all get out and introspective.

"Spill." She gestured at me grandly with her spatula like a good witch waving her wand.

"Tell me if this seems sketchy to you." I shared what I'd overheard and been told while she dished up two platters of varying items from more pastries to waffles to her delicious French bread. She finished when I did, handing me the plates which I balanced as she spoke.

"Sketchy beyond the ability to sketch further into sketchood," she said. "On all levels."

Thought so. "More importantly," I said, "why are Bonnie and Joyce suddenly so chummy when just last night they were mortal enemies over the man who cheated on them both?"

"I don't know, Fee," Daisy blinked her big eyes at me, "but I know someone who is going to dig until she finds out." Her wink and huge smile made me laugh.

Smartass bestie.

I turned to deliver the food, only to find Bonnie standing in the doorway of the kitchen. My mind spun as I tried to figure out how long she'd been waiting there and just how much she'd heard while Daisy softly cleared her throat and turned back to the frying pan with a wicked grin on her face.

"Despite the fact it's none of your business who I work with, I know how this looks." For the first time since her crying jag last night, Bonnie didn't sound arrogant. If anything, regardless of the content of her words, she looked a bit deflated, worn out. She had no problem meeting my eyes, though, as if to show me she didn't have anything to hide.

"You're right," I said. "Your business is your business. Unless you killed your husband." She never flinched. "Because that would be the sheriff's business."

"Especially if I hired Joyce to commit the murder," she said. Nodded. "I'm aware of that, Fiona. But this entire incident has opened my eyes to a few truths I've had to accept." She squared her shoulders, British accent deepening as if she rewound herself before my eyes, to an earlier time when perhaps she was more optimistic and less materialistic. "I'm done being angry all the time, I suppose. I ran into Joyce this morning, and something just snapped." She tossed her hands, smiled ever so faintly, like a real person lived in her heart. Didn't make her innocent, but it certainly went a long way to softening my image of her, for what that was worth.

"Fair enough," I said, drifting past her. She took one of the platters from me but didn't follow, forcing me to stop and wait for her to speak again.

"I wanted to ask you about the man in the garden last night. Malcolm Murray, was it?" She glanced at Daisy then hastily moved through the door, into the hall outside the dining room. But she didn't enter, keeping her voice down as I joined her. "Should I be worried for my physical safety?"

Right. She probably didn't have much contact with mob types in her world. "I don't know," I said. Thought about it a moment. "If not from him, then whoever hired him to collect, yes." She paled again, knuckles whitening as her fingers tightened on the edges of the platter. Just what I needed, for her to break another of my grandmother's china pieces. Selfish? Oh, yes. "I'd go to the police, if you're willing to risk taking it through legal channels." Good catch, Fee. Because I certainly hadn't contemplated suggesting the woman pay off her husband's bookie. Surely doing so was against the law or something.

Bonnie's hands clasped the platter in such a death grip I wondered if she'd break it in half from the pressure of using it as her gravity. Seriously? The damages would be added to her bill. "When he threatened me, when I found out Ron had gambled away and cheated the government out of so much money… I spoke to his accountant this morning." She shuddered faintly. "I missed so much he was doing behind my back, distracted by the infidelities he let me see." She seemed to gather nerve, rushing on. "It made many things clearer. That I'd held onto the past for too long. That it was time to just move on rather than waiting for things to arrange themselves into perfection before I did anything." Bonnie smiled a bit again, softening further until her eyes shone with it. "I realized I'd been staying in one place out of fear. That if Ron hadn't died, I never would have divorced him."

"Um." I winced.

"Yes," she said, "yet another reason I'd want him dead. Except, I didn't know when he was alive what I know now that he's gone." She wrinkled her nose and laughed a little. "Did that make sense?"

It did. And, despite the circumstantial evidence against her—at least in my mind—she was moving further and further from the guilty department and firmly into unhappy widow who had every right to hate her dead husband without actually offing him status.

"So, you have no idea how long Ron was having money problems?" I shifted the platter of cooling French bread to both hands, the heat from the bottom making my balancing palm sweat.

"Years," she said, biting at her lower lip. "If his

accountant's confession is any indication. I wish I'd known. I might have divorced him long ago. Or not." She shrugged like it didn't matter anymore. "Now I wish I hadn't been so greedy and just walked away. He didn't deserve me." Chin up, she turned and walked into the dining room with the tray held high. I followed her, setting mine down on the buffet while Joyce rose to help herself, Bonnie relieving herself of her burden before grabbing a plate and piling it with fruit and pastries.

"You were asking about Ron's gambling." Joyce flinched, clearly guilty she'd been eavesdropping, but it was going around so I just nodded while Bonnie turned to listen. "There were rumors, as much about betting on horses as his infidelity." She hesitated, reaching out one hand to touch Bonnie's arm. "I'm sorry."

Her new best friend just shook her head. "Disappointing. But I suppose he was a cheating liar to begin with, so why not add insult to injury?"

"I can't believe I ever…" Joyce choked on her words while Bonnie moved in to rub her back in soothing circles. I couldn't help the climb of my eyebrows into my hairline at the scene. I mean, come on. Sure, her remorse looked real enough, but the fact Ron's widow soothed his former mistress with fresh kindness, and, "There, there, dear," seemed a bit farfetched.

People were so weird.

"I know the sheriff is going to ask," I said, "if he hasn't already. But where were you two when Ron was killed?" Was it just the night before last? If Dr. Aberstock was right and he'd been struck on the back of the head with a pot, anyone could have had the strength and reach to smother him, including these two. The fact he was sitting at the judge's counter in his seat told me whoever killed him knew him, likely lured him there. Someone he was comfortable with.

Like his wife. Or his former mistress.

"I'm a bit embarrassed to say I was rather drunk." Bonnie stopped rubbing Joyce's back, faint queasy smile on her face. Assumptions confirmed, then. "A nice young server kept bringing me bottles. You can check with him." She looked down at her narrow hands. "I believe I was on number three when you found Ron's body."

Pretty solid, and, from what I remembered of her condition when she arrived on the set and even later, here at Petunia's, I'd already accepted she'd been intoxicated. She'd been slurring her words, staggering, almost falling. Less grief-stricken and more blasted out of her mind. The memory of the wine on her breath almost gagged me.

"I tried to sneak back in, but hotel security kicked me out." Joyce hugged herself during her own recount of her whereabouts. "I guess Dale must have alerted them I was in the building. I think he was just trying to protect me. He's such a nice young man."

I'd ask him, but I'd already seen him interacting with Joyce the morning of the murder, escorting her off the set, so that sounded right to me. Still, wouldn't hurt to check with Alicia and see if her story checked out.

"One thing though," Joyce said, perking a bit. "I didn't think anything of it, but maybe it's important?" She met Bonnie's eyes before turning back to me. "When I was escorted off, I snuck in the back way, but that big man with the giant dog caught me." Bill Saunders and Moose. Another clarifying conversation to have. "When he was leading me away, I saw Clara exiting the back door of the sound stage." Bonnie gasped softly while Joyce nodded in response. "Maybe I was seeing things, because it was pretty dark, but when she passed under the light by the door, she looked like she was crying."

CHAPTER TWENTY-FOUR

Crew was on my mind when I helped Daisy clean up breakfast and not for the reason he lingered with me when I fell asleep the night before. I had more information for him. Of course, I did, right? But would he be as open and willing this morning as he had been when I left his house after that most amazing of kisses?

Well, regardless, I wasn't going to let lingering doubt over his response stop me. I'd already burned that bridge down and he'd still laughed when I giggled over our embrace and seemed open enough to exploring what we might feel like together. If he changed his mind again when I dug my freckled nose into places I shouldn't have, then maybe he was nuts and I really didn't want to be with him.

Excuses to be a busybody? Check.

When Bonnie and Joyce both left after 10AM, I abandoned Daisy once again with Petunia and headed for the Lodge. She didn't complain, bless her, but I saw her reaching for the pug's harness and booties as I slid out the door, so I was pretty sure she was planning a visit to my mother with the irresistible dog in tow. I really needed to join them and see if I could convince Mom to change her mind, but the lure of the mystery behind Ron Williams's murder shoved me behind the wheel and drove me, an unwilling partner, I swear, back up the mountain for the third day in a row.

As luck would have it, Bill was in Alicia's office when I poked my head in, the tall, lumbering maintenance man nodding with an affable smile while the slim blonde rose to hug me in greeting.

"Did you see the flooring?" Alicia squealed faintly. "Jared said it arrived."

"It's gorgeous." It took me a moment to realize she was talking about the wood floors for the annex. My mind wasn't on my business, was it? "You did an amazing job."

"I can't wait to see it installed," she said. Hesitated, smile fading from eager delight to sorrow. "Fee, I meant to mention yesterday and didn't, but Jared and I were just destroyed about how Lucy was treated." One hand fluttered at me, Bill grunting his agreement with a big scowl on his face. "Is she okay?"

I sidestepped the question with a shrug. "Mind if

I ask a favor?"

Her hurt for Mom morphed into a rueful expectation. "I knew it. You're not here for sympathy or annex small talk, are you? You want a look at my surveillance tapes." She winked broadly like I was asking something much more provocative. Was my snooping that transparent? Bill chuckled next to me, his gravelly voice rough but kind.

"Don't tease her like that," he said, winking at me. The ex-con had warmed up a great deal both to Alicia and her staff since he'd rescued me and saved my life almost a year ago. Maybe having Dad vet him and speak well of him helped, but I think it was more the fact Alicia was just a great manager. He didn't seem as standoffish and sad, at least, though the shadow of his loss and his guilt would always remain in the deep lines of his face.

Alicia linked arms with me, leading me into the large space behind the front desk, Bill trailing after us.

"Joyce Young tells me you caught her sneaking around the night of the murder." I addressed that to the maintenance man while Alicia sat down, delicate in her pencil skirt, and started the computer.

He frowned a bit, rubbed his stubbled chin. "I did catch someone poking about," he said. "Well, Moose did. She seemed pretty upset, but she left without a fight." He shrugged. "Not much to say about that."

"She mentioned she saw the show creator exiting the back door," I said. "That she was crying. Do you remember seeing Clara, too?"

Bill's frown deepened before he sighed. "I'm sorry, Fee," he said. "Maybe? That film crew is using the back entry like their own private way around this place." He sounded annoyed by the fact. "I've taken to leaving it open, so they don't set off the alarms all the time." No alarm meant the murderer could have snuck in and out easily, not that it was Bill's fault.

Alicia groaned as she turned toward me. "Poor Bill's been run off his feet getting things sorted for them." She leaned over and patted his hand with a beaming smile which he answered with an adorable grin. "You're a trooper and I'd be lost without you."

He actually blushed before coughing softly. "Just happy to have the job, ma'am."

Alicia wrinkled her nose at me. "Ma'am. Imagine."

I laughed while she returned to her monitor before making a small sound of discovery. "Here you go, Fee. And yes, I know exactly what you're looking for." She sat back as I leaned in to watch Moose and Bill corral Joyce, the camera at the perfect angle to catch the back door. "Just like Bill said." We all waited while the small image of Joyce seemed to argue a moment with him, time running at 5:23 and counting. When he guided her away, the door opened and, sure enough, Clara Clark exited, right at 5:25. She paused there a moment while Joyce and Bill departed, wiping at her face before stomping off toward the ski lifts.

"That much is true, then," I said. "What about

Bonnie Williams?" I already had my answer, or so I thought, but it didn't hurt to check.

"Crew looked into that already," Alicia said. "Turns out she was in her room, loaded drunk. One of my guys was running her wine that afternoon. I trust him, Fee. He has no reason to lie about her condition."

"Could she have faked how drunk she was?" Good alibi, that, though my personal encounters with her were enough for me. "Dumped the wine and maybe took the elevator down to the set, killed Ron, then gone back upstairs and pretended to be drunk?" Seemed possible, except Alicia was shaking her head, already back at the monitor.

"You can see," she said, pointing at the screen and the time, "that she never leaves her room. Here, I'll speed it up." She cued up another block of video, the screen now split in two between the back entrance and an interior corridor. She fast-forwarded and I watched as a few people passed the camera over the exit door of the floor, entering the view of the one at the elevator.

One was Patrice York who went to her room at about 2:45PM and didn't exit again. So, I could mark the host of the show off the list. As for Bonnie, not once did she emerge once she arrived around three, but the waiter was there at least three times. And the only other person to visit her door was Robert, and that wasn't until after 6:15PM, a quarter-hour past the time Crew arrived.

Okay, so she was off the hook, as was Joyce.

"Thanks, Alicia," I said, then smiled at the big man leaning over to look at the screen behind us. "And Bill. That's a load off my mind."

"Bonnie and Joyce are both at Petunia's?" Alicia didn't seem concerned by their defection to my business. "A handful, I bet."

"Actually, it's a funny story," I said. "They're going into business together." I paused then, eyes narrowing as I considered the last person on the top of my rapidly shrinking list. "What about Malcolm Murray?"

Alicia's eyebrows shot up. "He was here," she said. "But not that afternoon. In the morning."

When I'd seen him personally. "You're sure?" How did she know to check?

"Crew asked," she said. "He said you mentioned seeing him so…"

Well now. Crew did follow up on my information then, did he? Good to know.

"That leaves Clara," I said. "Though I have no idea why she'd want to kill one of her own judges."

"And the crew," Alicia said. "Not to mention the show host, Patrice." Alicia hadn't noted the host entering her room, I guess. Maybe I should inquire after her anyway? "And how about this year's leader, Molly Abbott?" I wasn't the only armchair detective in town. I grinned at her while she flushed. "What can I say? You're a terrible influence."

I was, at that.

"I'm pretty sure Molly isn't a suspect," I said while my eyes widened at the scene unfolding on the top right of Alicia's screen at the 5:31 timecode, six minutes after Clara's departure. And within the half-hour timeline of Ron's death, if Dr. Aberstock's estimation was correct. Alicia had left the feed from the back door running while we reviewed the upstairs hallway. Movement caught my attention while the very woman I'd just crossed off my list slipped out of the exit, looked both ways, then slunk off toward the ski lifts, the same direction Clara had gone.

I gaped at the sight for a long moment before exhaling. "Can you call Crew and tell him? No, never mind. I'll do it." Better for only one of us to get in trouble. He'd just blame me for encouraging bad behavior. Then again, she could claim she was just double-checking her feeds in case something came up. Still.

"He has copies of all of the footage," Alicia said, taking the pressure off. "He likely knows already."

Awesome. That meant I could keep poking around and not have to talk to him because he already knew what I knew, right?

Oh, Fee.

Thing was, I could have just left then and there. The two women I'd come to investigate had both been exonerated and Clara's exit was rather telling. But I hadn't expected the surge of anger at Molly, thinking she'd fooled me into liking her when she might be the murderer. I'd had enough trouble with misjudging people in the past, even almost fell for a killer because he was cute and showed interest. Never mind he was a former drug addict who then tried to strangle me when I found him out.

I'd had enough of being deceived. "Do you have Molly's room number handy?"

Alicia hesitated before sighing. "I'm staying out of this," she said, but not in a judging tone, more resigned and with a final twitch of a grin when she looked up the booking. "417. Be careful."

"She won't have to be," Bill rumbled. "I'll be right behind her."

I looked up at him, startled by the offer. "You don't have to come with me, Bill."

"You have this streak of stubbornness that leads to bad luck," he said, "no fault of yours. So, if I can have your back, I'm here."

"I'd feel a whole lot better if you didn't argue," Alicia said. Her reticence wasn't about me actually confronting Molly but worry about me? That I could appreciate.

"You're both lovely," I said. "But you also know where I'm going. If I don't come back down, call Crew." I was half-joking, though Bill looked like he wanted to fight me on it. "Seriously, she's harmless." Wasn't she harmless? "I'm just going to ask her a few questions, that's all."

Alicia rose and hugged me. "You're an idiot. Don't be a hero, Fee." She let me go, blinking. "Bill told me about the storm last year. Just, don't die on me, okay?" Her lower lip trembled. "Not on my watch."

There wasn't much I could do to reassure her and though I insisted he stay behind, I felt Bill watching me as I got on the elevator and didn't exhale until the doors closed. He'd probably take the stairs and hover, but I could live with that. Funny, how exactly did I manage to gather such amazing friends who cared what happened to me when all I did was bring them trouble?

Molly's door was a short walk from the elevator. I knocked while I tried to formulate the right way to approach my questions, hearing voices inside fall still before someone approached the door. When it opened, I shouldn't have been surprised to find Molly wasn't alone.

"Fiona," Dale said, blushing a bit as the young baker, standing further in the room near the bed, her hair a bit mussed and her cheeks pink patted at her clothes telling me I'd interrupted something decidedly naughty, "please, come in."

CHAPTER TWENTY-FIVE

The moment I entered, Dale waved at Molly. "I'll be going."

"Hang on," I said, "if you don't mind. I want to talk to you, too."

Dale hesitated but didn't run away, Molly frowning a bit, her embarrassment at my appearance during their make-out session clearly forgotten. "What's going on?"

I turned to her, reminding myself not to trust anyone despite the innocence on her face. Expressions could lie, after all. "Were you on the sound stage around the time Ron died?"

Dale made a strangling sound as Molly flushed deep red, but not a blush, more out of anger. Not at me, though. She waved off Dale who hurried to her side while she clamped her lips together a moment, sinking to the end of the bed.

"I was there," she said. "I saw Ron go in and I wanted to talk to him about Lucy. About Janet's cheating." She met Dale's eyes, not mine, as if convincing him. "He hit on me. I… I didn't know what to do."

"I warned you about him so many times," Dale said. Not accusing, comforting, though he looked guarded, then sad.

"I needed to know one way or another if he was going to speak out against Janet." She sagged in Dale's grasp, his arm around her shoulders. "I honestly couldn't take it anymore, Fee. I wanted to quit the show when I found out about the scandal. Clara convinced me to just ignore it, but when Janet was awarded a place in the special and your mother was sabotaged…" She sniffed softly, met my eyes at last, hers brimming. "This isn't the kind of show I want to win. Or be associated with."

I wasn't expecting integrity as an alibi. "Why did Clara let it go on? Surely it was bad for business."

"Not this business," Dale said, a bit harsher than necessary. "I already told you, controversy was one of the only things keeping this show afloat. Without it, the ratings plummet. Tell her, Moll. What Clara wanted you to do."

She leaned into him, voice tiny. "She wanted me to take a page from Janet's book and sabotage one of my competitors."

I was so over this whole gigantic mess. "Did you

see Clara talking to Ron when you got there?"

She nodded, wiping her nose with the heel of her hand. "They were arguing about something, I think the cookbook launch. At least, I heard him mention it before Clara stormed off. She was crying. Clara never cries." She wept herself then, head on Dale's shoulder. "I just want to bake. This is so much pressure. I hope the show does get canceled."

Hard not to feel for her, but still. "You realize you were there very close to the time the doctor said Ron was murdered?"

Molly stared at me with her giant eyes wide, her lips trembling. "I didn't know that," she said. "I wasn't thinking about anything after he… he…" She stumbled over her words. "I just ran."

I could have pressed her, but that wasn't my job. Crew needed to know she was at the top of the suspect pile with means, motive and opportunity. It felt horrible to leave the two of them, Dale comforting Molly, with a new destination in mind. Not Crew's office, not just yet. I needed to eliminate a couple of people first before I brought this to him. I was reaching for my phone to call Alicia for Clara's room number when the showrunner herself stepped off the elevator and headed toward me. And she wasn't alone. Patrice grabbed her arm, spun her around, said something too quiet for me to make out. The host met my eyes as Clara hung up her phone, not seeing me when she addressed the woman beside her.

"It's canceled," she snarled. "There, are you

happy now?"

Patrice's face scrunched up. "Like I didn't know that was coming." She almost spit that in her boss's face. "Why do you think I spent all afternoon yesterday on the phone with my agent?" That's why she was in her room and didn't emerge until after the murder was discovered. "I'm already in the market for a new gig. Because working with you has been nothing but a nightmare." She spun and stomped off, tossing her hands while Clara glared after her. The showrunner didn't notice I was there until I was at her elbow and jumped a bit when she turned and saw me standing next to her.

"Your show?" I tried for sympathetic despite not really liking her very much at the moment. Not only was she possibly a murderer—she could have gone back to the set after Molly left—but she perpetrated crimes against contestants with the moral code of a slug.

Sorry, slugs. Didn't mean to offend with the comparison.

"And with it the damned cookbook launch." She was tied to that, too, was she? Clara's round cheeks darkened, faint veins showing as if she'd lost her temper one too many times and burst the capillaries beneath her skin. "Everything's ruined."

"A man is dead," I said, knowing I came across cold and that maybe Ron Williams didn't deserve the kind of respect I figured she should be showing. "A woman who cheated her way to the top of your little game got to benefit from her crime and you're worried about your show?"

"Of course, I am!" Clara looked at me like I was the one who lost my mind, not the other way around. "This was my baby, my creation. And it's ruined, thanks to Ron Damned Williams."

Hello, Suspect. Nice to meet you.

"The network is sick of controversy," she said, staring at her phone. "His death put an end to their support. And that means I'm shut down unless I can find another broadcaster to take me on."

"Is that what you two were fighting about just before he died?" She didn't seem the type to spill her soul when someone asked a question, but I had her off balance. "What made you cry?"

She flinched as if being caught crying was a crime in itself. Maybe in her line of work it was. "I already told that sheriff of yours when I left Ron, he was alive and whining. As usual. Asking for more money, surprise, surprise." She inhaled, pulling herself under control again. "I wanted him to rein in Janet, but he convinced me otherwise. And I was desperate enough when her cheating raised the ratings to try it again this season. But Molly wouldn't play. And no one would believe it of her anyway." She seemed to deflate just slightly, a woman with a mission adrift for the first time in years. "He refused to help, told me he was planning to leave at the end of the season and start his own show. That would mean the end of mine. So yeah, I cried over a baby I'd birthed and raised the last eleven years." She seemed close to tears again before shaking them off. "Ron's death means the death of my show. Why would I kill him?"

That much at least rang true. "Any idea where his cookbook came from?" She stared at me a moment in surprise. "Bonnie doesn't seem to have any idea."

"Ron didn't tell his so-called wife anything." But Clara frowned, shook her head. "I have no idea. I never asked. Didn't care. He just seemed to snap it out of thin air about three months ago, no mention of it beforehand. The launch was going to wrap the season, raise the ratings. Branch us into cooking, not just baking for next season." I hadn't heard that. "Why he was so popular, though, I could never understand." She grunted something under her breath that sounded like "poser." "Frankly, I never considered him that smart or a very good baker. His rep was all press release and ancient history. He hadn't picked up a spatula in years."

"Have you tasted any of the recipes?" What did the cookbook have to do with this? Anything, or was I grasping at roux and pork tenderloin?

She shrugged. "I heard they were good."

Talk about a glowing recommendation. But wait, did she seem uncomfortable with the reference to his cookbook? I wondered why and instead blundered forward, seeing I was losing her focus as she stared at her phone as if considering something. Because hitting suspects with a rapid-fire pile of uncomfortable questions usually got me what I wanted to know. "And his gambling issues? His trouble with the IRS?"

She flinched, shook her head. Didn't answer. So,

she knew and did nothing yet again? "I wonder if I'm too late to pitch that other show for the fall."

Moving on, then.

When Clara looked up at me again, she was already dialing. "Listen, I'm sorry about your mother, that she got caught up in all this. But the show's over and whoever killed Ron, it wasn't me. If you'll excuse—Perry! Yeah, you heard, too. All good, I have that new pitch I wanted to…" her voice drifted off as she hurried away, head down, talking to whoever it was she figured could get her career back on track.

While I pondered what I'd learned, heading for the lobby with about as many questions and answers as I came with.

CHAPTER TWENTY-SIX

I didn't make it far, stumbling on Bill who lurked, as I'd expected he would, near the elevators when I emerged downstairs. At least he didn't follow me all the way up, but the relief on his face when I stepped out into the noisy lobby made me smile.

I hooked my arm through his as I guided him down the hall toward the staff quarters. "I'm fine, see?"

"Good to know," he said. "Any luck?"

"Not sure." I stopped him beside the exit sign over the doors I'd been pushed through on Valentine's Day, staring at them and trying not to remember the bitter cold and my near death from exposure. "But I could use some insight."

"Anything." He glanced at the doors himself.

"Let me guess, you're wondering about ways into and out of the dining room?"

Clever man. "So, there are the main ones into the lobby," obviously, "and the side door that leads to this hallway," I pivoted and pointed at the one beside us. "Any others?"

"One more," he said. "This way." He led me into the quiet of the partially collapsed sound stage, around the back of the set past the green room area and to the far wall to the right of the main entrance. I had no idea there was a separate hallway back here, nor that it had a staircase attached. But when he opened the plain, gray door, nondescript but clearly an exit, I looked up the cold, basic concrete steps with a faint frown.

"No camera," I said.

He pursed his lips, turned on his heel as he checked out the view above us. "Nope."

Which meant this investigation was far from over. "Crew know about this?"

Bill paused, head tilted much like his big dog would if he heard an odd noise. "Now that you mention it, I don't think so."

Hmmm. "Where does this come out?"

"Exits on every floor," he said. "Mostly for maintenance."

Well, craptastic. "So, if the killer found this door, they could have used it and no one would be the wiser."

He nodded, looked contrite. "Should have thought of that."

"You're not a criminal, Bill," I said. "Why would you?"

His slow smile lit his craggy face like I'd handed him the keys to the town.

I left the Lodge with a lot of thinking to do, heading for my car while texting instructions for Alicia to check any cameras close to the newly discovered exit. She promised she'd forward anything she found to Crew while I applauded myself for a job well done. See, I could play ball with him. I didn't even ask for the information for myself, did I?

Way to cover tracks and call it a win, Fee.

I filled in Daisy on everything I found while she fed Petunia an early lunch.

"I spent the morning researching the cookbook," she said, turning her laptop around to show me what she'd found. The home screen for a large bookstore chain showed the cover with Ron's face plastered front and center, the *Cake or Break Bread* title making me eye-roll. There were a large number of reviews already, though from the flag next to the purchase button it was still on preorder and wasn't due to be released until April when the show was supposed to wrap.

"Looks like a lot of happy reviewers for a book that's not out yet," I said.

"Well, publishers do prerelease ARCs to early readers to drum up interest," Daisy said. Blushed when I arched an eyebrow at her in the know. "I'm on the list for advance reader copies from Purely Paranormal Press."

Right, she loved those witchy books. Huh, but I had no idea there was such a thing. "So, anyone on the list gets the book, a chance to read it," or try the recipes in this case, "and leave a review before the book is published?"

"Exactly." She pointed at the list of five stars, a handful of four stars, but not a bad review in sight. "Funny thing is, usually there are a few bad apples if you'll pardon the food comparison. This many raving reviews? Smells like yesterday's fish."

Interesting. "So, is there a way to look at the sample? Test one of the recipes?"

"Sometimes," she said. "But not in this case. And there are big-name chefs in the list of reviewers, either. That makes me wonder, Fee."

"If, like Ron Williams himself, this book is all hype?" Made sense. But was it reason to murder him? If the book was a fraud, for example, could someone have found out? I found it hard to believe someone would kill over some recipes, but odder things had crossed my path. From the crazy way the show was run, maybe death by designer dish wasn't so farfetched after all.

I heard the front doorbell chime but was too slow to get it, Daisy already on the move as I perused the book page, reading reviews that sounded just a bit too flowery and excited. Fakes? Possibly. Reinforcing my suppositions about the book's authenticity.

I turned when I heard the kitchen door swish, caught the warning look on Daisy's face just before my gaze slipped past her and settled on Vivian

French. The sudden urge to leap at her and tear her hair out hit me so hard it froze me in place, both from shock at the reaction and horror that I gave her that kind of power over me.

In the silence that ensued, Vivian spoke.

"I'm not here for you," she said, voice firm but low. "I'm here for Lucy."

"To take another shot at her?" I found my own voice apparently. "Tell her she'd be better off working for you than being her own person?"

Daisy looked shocked, then pissed. So, Mom hadn't told her the details of Vivian's attack, either? Shouldn't have comforted me as much as it did, but I was jealous of my mother like that, I guess.

Did Vivian actually flinch ever so slightly? Her already porcelain skin paling further? Must have been the camel wool of her coat clashing with her skin tone. Because surely, she wasn't showing a breath of humanity.

"Your mother was wronged," she said. Stiffened as I opened my mouth to tell her where she could take her platitudes. "I like to win, Fee. But not that way. Fraud is a hollow victory."

She'd rather wipe up the floor with my mother fair and square? Didn't make her a good person.

"Whatever," I said. "You have a point?"

Daisy cut in before Vivian's flushing response could turn to an argument like the one we'd carried out in the back alley of her bakery. That had been productive if yelling and screaming like little kids in a playground got us anywhere.

My bestie took the reins, gesturing for Vivian to join us. "It took a lot for you to come here," she said, soft and understanding while I fought the urge to make a face. "You found something you wanted to share?"

Vivian tsked at Daisy as if her tone offended, before striding forward and setting her own laptop on the already cluttered counter. I made no move to give her space and she ended up hip-to-hip with me, the clash of the computers unfolding as hers butted up against mine.

"I have some connections in the cookbook world," she said like that wasn't the most hilarious thing to come out of anyone's mouth ever. I almost giggled as she went on. "I convinced one of them to forward me their ARC." She clicked on a file on her computer desktop, the background a shot of the bakery in summer. It was actually really pretty. Grumble. I guess I needed to hire a photographer to shoot Petunia's and the annex.

Distractions. Got to love them.

"Did you try the recipes?" Daisy had joined us, pinning Vivian between us.

"I didn't have to," the arrogant blonde said, manicured fingernails clicking on her keyboard. "One look through the pages and I knew the truth."

"Let me guess," I said, "the book is a fraud." I was so clever I could kiss myself.

Which made me think of Crew's lips and grin all over again.

"Actually," Vivian startled me by saying, "they're

all fantastic. The combinations are wonderful, I've used some myself in the past."

"How could you?" Daisy met my eyes as Vivian scrolled through the list of recipes, stopping at one for some kind of stew. "The book hasn't come out yet."

"Oh," Vivian said, a happy tone of malice running through her voice, "but it has. At least, the individual recipes have." She minimized the file window and clicked another, side-by-siding the two recipes while I skimmed the ingredients and the instructions. The one from the book was typed up, formatted perfectly while the other looked as if it was a scanned copy of a typewritten page.

"Stolen?" Daisy likely didn't know she gasped when she said that word like some startled heroine in one of her paranormal romance novels. Adorable.

Vivian shrugged, paging down the book again before clicking another file and repeating the performance. Another scanned page, another recipe plagiarized. "I've seen the advanced reviews. None of them call out the theft. Perhaps the reviewers are unfamiliar with the source. But I'm not." She sounded pissed. "He might have thought he could get away with it, though. The creator is obscure and now passed away."

Did that negate the copyright? No, it would just transfer to next of kin, right? But it might have made Ron brave enough to take the risk if there wasn't anyone to claim ownership. Still, the padded reviews made me think he was doing his best to keep his fraud under wraps until the book actually published. Could he really benefit from the release financially if he was exposed?

Maybe the money from the sale of the book wasn't what he'd been after. Publishers paid advances, didn't they? And he was in need of funds if Malcolm's visit was any indication.

"That's worth murdering over," I said out loud.

"Exactly what I was thinking," Vivian said.

"Whose recipes are they?" A name was scrawled at the bottom, but I couldn't read the writing.

"Someone familiar," Vivian said, closing both windows and clicking the last link. "I met her a long time ago, an old friend of the family. I started watching *Cake or Break* because she was in the first season, back when they brought in-home cooks with real talent." That better not have been a jab at Mom. The video came on, playing the opening sequence. Vivian pushed the slider past it to the middle of the show and an older woman in glasses and a cute floral dress, portly but beaming, while next to her, scowling at the judges, stood none other than Ron Williams.

"Wait, he was a contestant?" I had no idea. "How long has the show been on?"

"This is the eleventh season," Daisy said while Vivian spoke over her.

"He won that first round, despite inferior baking," she said. Her bias wasn't showing or anything. "The prize was a place at the judging table. It should have gone to her." She pointed at the older woman. Why did she look like someone I knew? "He won by cheating, at least, that was the rumor. But she refused to challenge him and went home to her family, taking her amazing recipes with her. Yet again as unknown as she had been all along despite her genius." She actually sounded sad for the woman.

"I'm sorry for your friend," I said. "But you do realize this doesn't look good, Vivian. Crew will have questions."

She snapped the lid of her laptop shut, crossing her arms over her chest, scowling at me. "Why do you think I'm here? It seems his tastes are leaning toward the more provincial," one carefully shaped eyebrow rose as she looked me up and down, "but if you have his ear, you can pass this along."

"And be the one to get in trouble for snooping," I said. "Thanks a lot."

She hesitated, dropped her hands to her sides, staring at her closed laptop. "Gloria died in obscurity," she said. "When she should have been a star. But she didn't want that for herself. Wouldn't want it for her granddaughter, either. I can't believe she doesn't know what Ron did to her grandmother's family recipes."

Wait, what? Who were we talking about exactly? I must have said that out loud because Vivian exhaled with an irritation that was much more like her than the woman I'd been talking to the last few minutes.

"Gloria Kingsley," she said. "Molly Abbott is her granddaughter."

CHAPTER TWENTY-SEVEN

Wow, that was a bombshell to drop. While I sorted out the implications—and Molly's return to susptecthood—Daisy spoke up.

"Isn't there anything she can do? To shut down the book?" She seemed more upset about it than Vivian. It did answer the copyright question. All ownership should have passed to Molly, at least as far as I knew.

The cold blonde shrugged, her coat sighing around her. "There are copyright laws," she said. "But if Gloria never registered them, Ron could have dragged out a court case until the family couldn't afford to fight any longer."

"Actually," I said, "he was in financial trouble himself."

She met my eyes, crystal blue surprised. "Really. How interesting."

I felt myself still in that moment as I realized just how alike the two of us were. And that, if circumstances were different, Vivian and I might—might, in an alternate universe I never wanted to visit—have been friends.

Shudder.

"Regardless," she said, gathering her computer and sliding it into the designer bag draped over her arm, depositing a thumb drive on the counter with careful precision, "if someone did kill him over the stolen recipes, I wanted to share what I knew."

"Thank you." I meant it. And Daisy was right, it had to have taken a lot for Vivian to come here like this.

She pursed her lips, jaw working before her gaze snapped to mine again. "I had nothing to do with your mother's sabotage."

"I know," I said. "Pretty sure it was Janet."

She blew a soft raspberry, tension releasing, though her arrogant carriage of confident poise never left her. "That one. Surely this whole disaster will expose her for the fraud she is." Vivian actually sounded offended. "She's a terrible representation of our business." She half-turned to go then stopped and faced me again. "Please tell Lucy how sorry I am for what happened." There was real regret in her face, in her voice. "I should have realized she would never present such a terrible finished product. She's too professional for that."

Wow, that was high praise. "I'll tell her," I said. "But it would mean more coming from you."

Vivian blinked. "She won't want to talk to me."

The last thing I needed was to find empathy for her, but it woke up anyway and I relented.

"Try her, Vivian," I said. "I think you'll be surprised. And rather than offering her a job, maybe you'd consider some kind of cooperative effort. Mom's not just a fantastic baker. She's brilliant."

Vivian didn't say anything to that, but she did look like her mind was spinning. She left without another word, side-stepping Petunia who panted at her feet, grinning up at her in her happy pug way. The blonde actually stumbled before hurrying out, Daisy leaning against the counter and watching her go with a low, sharp whistle.

"I never thought I'd see the day Fiona Fleming and Vivian French had civil words for each other." She winked at me. "That was surreal. We should buy a lottery ticket."

Made me snort. And release some of the animosity I'd held toward Vivian all these years. Honestly, I had to give her kudos. She'd taken a small-town business and built it into a bit of an empire for herself. If I was going to be honest, too, I had to ask myself how much of her arrogance was pomposity and how much was loneliness?

Then again, it would burn her butt to know I thought she might be lonely. Yeah, still a little bitter.

"Weird being a grownup, Daisy," I said.

She hugged me, let me go with a beaming smile.

"Silly," she said, "you know the rules."

"Never grow up," we said together.

I grabbed my laptop and the thumb drive and headed for the door while my bestie laughed when I paused, wincing.

"Just go," she said. "Let me know if you need bail money."

Crap, I forgot to fill her in on the kiss. Seemed like terrible timing. "Remind me to tell you something when I get home," I said. "And thanks, Day. I won't be long."

Crew was in his office when I arrived at the station. Robert was conspicuously absent. On guard duty at the Lodge? Jill grinned at me when I entered, Toby standing to hug me. I embraced the receptionist with a squeeze of my own, the soft fleece of her vest a constant.

"I'll see if he's able to talk," Toby said, a determined look on her face. Before she could cross the hardwood floor to the swinging gate that separated the bullpen from the reception area, Crew's voice called out from his open door.

"I know it's you, Fiona. Just come in."

He didn't sound mad, so I took that as a good sign, along with the thumbs up from Toby and the headshake from Jill. Crew looked up as I passed the threshold of his doorway, gesturing for me to take a seat with his pen before looking down at the pile of paperwork in front of him. I closed the door behind me, sank into the creaking wooden chair that was far too familiar for someone who really shouldn't be visiting a sheriff's office as often as I did.

"I'll be right with you," he said. Looked up again, met my eyes, his friendly but guarded. "I take it you're not here for a beer."

I almost let out my inner smart ass. So close to quipping about wanting another kiss I had to clench my abdomen against the need to giggle. "Not a beer." Oh, dear. That smoldering tone was almost bad enough.

Crew's lips quirked in a grin, and he looked down. Was that a flush on his cheeks? I know mine were pretty hot. I shed my coat while he signed the bottom of the paper in front of him and filed it in a drawer in his desk before sliding it shut and leaning back in his chair, tossing his pen to the surface.

"Okay, Fiona Fleming," he said. "Kiss me."

It took me about four seconds to realize he actually said, "Hit me," not "Kiss me," and in that time I gaped at him while his smile faded and he cocked his head to one side, crease forming between his eyebrows.

"You okay?" He sat forward while I remembered to inhale.

"All good," I squeaked. "Sorry, brain fart, never mind. Here." I slammed my laptop down on his desk. "I snooped." At least he seemed amused. "With help."

"Nice to know you're now recruiting other townsfolk to dig into police business." Crew's sarcasm was cut with humor. "What have you got?"

I ended up scooting around to his side of the

desk, tucking my chair in close and walked him through what Vivian showed me, Daisy's investigation into the review process and everything I'd learned today about Molly, Clara and Joyce.

"I can't help but come back around to Molly," I said, watching the images of Gloria Kingsley as she presented her food to the judges.

Crew nodded, eyes glued to the screen. He was so close to me his shoulder brushed mine, the scent of his aftershave not overpowering, but enough to tickle my nose. When he turned his head to meet my eyes, his lips were uncomfortably accessible.

"Malcolm Murray's bookie friend is out of state," he said. "I'm waiting on cooperation from Boston PD and the FBI. But I highly doubt he'd kill Ron over a debt he was collecting for someone else."

"Bonnie and Joyce both seem to have solid alibis," I said. "Wait, the side stairs." I told him about Bill's reveal and Crew frowned, rubbing the faint stubble on his chin with one big hand while he stared at nothing. "I asked Alicia to review any footage from the area, so she might be sending you more security tapes."

"Good catch, Fee." He actually sounded like he meant it. Something warm and soft burst in my chest while I did my best not to wriggle like a puppy told she was a good girl. Because I was not that woman, thank you. "Clara's still a person of interest. It's her show and she's been running it since the beginning. She had to have known about Ron's recipe theft. That the cookbook is plagiarized."

Was that why she acted uncomfortably when I asked her about it? "Or she found out and knew he was about to ruin her once and for all." She'd been eager to pitch a new show to the network that dropped *Cake or Break*. I could only imagine scandal of any kind would ruin her chances.

"I'll have another talk with her." He sat back then, and I missed the nearness of him immediately.

"I find it so hard to imagine he could get away with stealing Gloria's recipes like that." My sense of fair play stirred a self-righteousness that startled me.

"Bringing us back to Molly." Crew tapped his fingers on the arms of his chair, rocking backward in a slow rhythm I found hypnotic. "And the suspicious timing of her departure from the set." He gestured at the screen in front of us. "Vivian's copies are all scans, so there's proof of their existence. So, Molly would have had a case against Ron. Still, she's probably right about the lawyer thing."

Just sucked someone could steal her grandmother's work like that. And triggered that further question I thought I had an answer to already.

"Why would Ron risk being caught for plagiarism anyway?" Had to be money, didn't it? "He must have been paid some kind of advance on the sales. But Malcolm was still looking. So, where's the money?"

"Ah, that I have an answer for." Crew leaned forward, fishing out a few pages from the file in front of him. "Ron Williams was being investigated by the IRS for tax evasion."

And I'd forgotten to mention I knew that already.

When I didn't react the way he expected to his supposed scoop of information, Crew sighed with rueful understanding. "Maybe he paid them off rather than a bookie?" Not so smart. The IRS might take his house, but Malcolm's bullies would have eventually broken his kneecaps. At least, I imagined so. Still, it was good to know I was right, that the sales of the cookbook weren't his aim. He'd chosen to publish in an effort to raise capital to cover part of his debt, though his lack of planning for what might happen after his fraud was discovered lowered my estimation of the man further.

As for Malcolm's plan to extract what was owed, the next time I talked to him, I'd ask him what his standard operating procedure was. Snort.

"I also found out Ron tried to launch a show of his own." Crew grinned when my surprise showed. I knew he'd been talking about one, thanks to Clara, but launching it? That was news. "Ah, so you *don't* know everything I know. That's gratifying."

Smartass sheriff. Good thing he was hot.

"The question remains, why did he die?" I ticked off reasons on my fingertips. "Infidelity?"

Crew shrugged. "I'm sure he had affairs with more than Joyce and Janet. The show was on for a long time."

Way to add more suspects to the pool. "Stolen recipes?"

"Molly." Crew nodded while my mind expanded cookbook suspicions to Bonnie and Clara. Bonnie because, as his wife, she'd be sucked into legal proceedings when and if Ron was sued and Clara because he was launching the book on her show.

"And financial problems?" The least likely, in my opinion, but still on the list. "Anything else?"

"How about being a reprehensible human being?" Crew sighed, toying with his pen. "Sorry. The more I dig into this guy, the less I like him. Not that liking him is a requirement to solving his murder. But."

Yeah. But.

He met my eyes then, blue sparkling. "That all you got?"

I shrugged, closing my computer. "Best I could do on short notice."

Crew leaned forward, nice and close again, only this time he seemed to do it on purpose, with purpose. A slow smile, kind of a smirk, truth be told, spread over his wide mouth as he came almost nose-to-nose with me.

"Anything else I can do for you, detective?" Was it just me or was that a suggestion in his voice? An invitation to something rather personal and altogether naughty that had me quivering inside.

Who knows what I might have said or done next? I have a feeling it would have ended in an embarrassing make-out session neither of us would live down. Except, of course, fate had a funny way of having my back when I really wished it would leave me alone and just live with the consequences of finding out what might happen if Crew kissed me again.

The soft knock was all the warning we got, followed almost immediately by Toby poking her head in. I whipped away from Crew, felt the heat on my cheeks burning while he backed away from me just as fast. The pair of us must have looked like we were up to something, but Toby had the good grace not to comment. She grinned, though.

"Alicia is calling from the Lodge," she said. "That woman's been at her again to strike the set." Didn't need two guesses to identify "that woman" as Clara Clark.

Crew sighed, stood, waited a long moment for me to get the point and leap to my feet, too.

"Thanks, Fee," he said. "I'll see you later?" Was there more than just courtesy in that question? Was it an invitation? I needed to stop asking myself dumb questions and reading things into other people that didn't exist.

That's why I found myself walking home, hugging my laptop, wishing Toby had just given us one more second alone.

CHAPTER TWENTY-EIGHT

I was surprised to run into Janet Taylor heading up the steps and into the sheriff's office, almost running her over in my distraction. She caught herself before I could bump her, scowling at me while I blinked into the sunshine.

"Sorry," I said. "Didn't see you there." Not sorry, though. Wished she'd fallen. Because I was a terrible person with Mommy protection issues.

Her pinched expression didn't lighten up. "I'm sure you did," she snapped. "Excuse me."

"Wait a second." I grasped for her arm but didn't touch her, catching myself at the last second. I did not need a crazy assault charge against me right now. Oddly, just the motion seemed to stop her as she tried to look down her narrow nose at me despite the fact I had a few inches on her.

"If you're going to accuse me of ruining your mother's baking, go ahead." She sniffed, cold air misting out of her lips as she spoke again. "But I'm the one who's been sabotaged here! Your mother doesn't have a nationally recognized reputation to uphold, does she?"

Talk about a puffed-up piece of work. "That gave you the right to dose Mom's sugar with salt, did it?" She was lucky I was clinging to my laptop and didn't have my hands free.

"She should have tasted her batter." Was she honestly smirking?

"Sounds like you needed to take your own advice," I shot back.

Janet's nasty demeanor faded just a bit. "I did," she snapped. "Whatever was in my mix, and I can guess from how hard my bake turned out..." she exhaled, anger returning. "We'll see if your sheriff is interested in justice or not."

I let her go, hoping Crew bounced her butt out into the cold. Like he could do anything about the disaster that was *Cake or Break*. But it left me with an interesting tidbit of curiosity to look up when I got home.

Daisy and Petunia were gone when I arrived back at the B&B, Joyce and Bonnie both out. I'd hoped to ask Joyce what Janet was talking about and instead resorted to my favorite investigative snoop tool, a search engine.

It wasn't long before I came up with the answer,

or what I guessed was the answer. The only ingredient that I could come up with that was odorless, tasteless and in powder form, that could harden a cake without being detectible with a quick taste test of raw batter was gelatin. But how to prove it? That was another story.

I checked the messages as I went over my bookings for the first of February and was surprised to find one from Alicia.

"Called Crew, but thought you should know." She sounded hurried, like she was walking somewhere, din of voices in the background. "Good call on the other exit door. Someone else was in the dining room, but I couldn't make out who. Emailed you the short clip from the camera at the front of the room, but it's pretty blurry because of the distance. We originally dismissed it because no live on the full set, too much crap in the way. I'll tell Crew when he gets here. Bye!"

My fingers fumbled on the keyboard of my computer while I quickly scanned my email for the message and opened it. The short video she sent seemed to take forever to load, but when it finally did, I understood what she meant. All the lights and the tall walls of the set blocked the actual murder scene from the camera. But there was enough space between the fake side of the set and the real wall I could make out the door to the maintenance stairs. I peered at the grainy, dark image taken all the way across the large space and I felt a shudder run through me before I frowned.

I knew exactly who that was, distance or not. Had privately thought this particular suspect cleared despite reservations about their possible guilt and motive for murder. I checked the time stamp and confirmed the death window. That the wavering figure who slipped through the side door with something cylindrical clutched in hand, hurrying onto the set did so at 5:36PM. I'd seen canisters like that in Mom's show kitchen, full of baking ingredients. Could this particular one have been cut with gelatin, perhaps?

For a brief moment, I almost let it go. Crew was there at the Lodge and would be viewing the clip himself. Surely, he'd recognize the person in the video and ask the appropriate questions.

Wouldn't he?

Only one way to find out. But first, I needed to confirm something I'd been told, something I should trust but wanted to make sure wasn't misleading or untrue. That led me on an internet hunt for a certain name and ties to a particular family while I tried to convince myself my suspicions were totally baseless.

They weren't. The information I had was accurate and the damning image of the figure at the maintenance stairs door gave me reason to doubt myself to the core one more time.

At least I had what I needed to hand Crew the case and maybe win me another kiss… as long as I wasn't misreading him as much as everyone else I thought I could trust. Sigh. I headed for the front door, swinging my coat around me, locking the house behind me. Terrible business practice? You betcha. But I was enough my father's daughter I couldn't just sit on the sidelines. Crew was right, I was born for this, like it or not.

I'd deliver my evidence in person. And if he already knew what I knew? Awesome. At least I'd be there to see justice done.

It was a tense, short drive to the mountain, a quick text to Daisy gaining me a reply I ignored as I drove up the winding road again. When I pulled into the parking lot, I hesitated over messaging Crew to warn him and decided against it. Not because I purposely wanted to keep him out of it. But because the sight of a tall, broad-shouldered former sheriff exiting his truck with a pink-haired woman at his side, the pair heading for the front doors drew my attention more so even than catching a murder.

I reached Dad as he passed through the glass doors, grabbing his arm and dragging him to the side of the lobby in the shade of a fake plant, glaring up at him while Clara, his companion, seemed to sense this was terrible timing to interrupt and headed off on her own before I could stop her.

"Dad," I snapped, watching the showrunner disappear into the crowd, heading for the elevators, "where have you been?"

He looked uncomfortable, like he would rather be anywhere other than here with me, facing me like this. I'd accused him of cheating on Mom before, with Alicia, of all people. Turned out she was his CI against Pete Wilkins. And here I was thinking terribly of him again, about this Siobhan Doyle woman and now with a quiver of doubt he'd been with Clara. I obviously still harbored a lot of trust issues over Ryan's infidelity for my mind to take me to such dark places, knowing how much Dad loved Mom. Still.

He had a lot to answer for, apparently.

"Fee," he said, shuffling his feet like an errant schoolboy. "What are you doing here?"

"Weak, Dad," I snapped. "No deflecting. Where's Mom?"

He looked even more contrite. "Home," he said.

"Alone," I said. "Like she's been since the morning of the damned show. You've been missing a lot, Dad. She needs you." Never mind my guilt Mom probably needed me, too, and I was just as bad running around investigating a murder I didn't need to poke my nose into because Crew would recognize the figure in the video—and the purpose of the canister carried on set—and I was wasting my time coming here.

Dad didn't seem to realize I was judging myself as much as him. He cleared his throat in an awkward kind of way that startled me. My father was the picture of cool cucumbers with a huge dose of stoic silence thrown in to season the mix. So, what could possibly make him look like he'd been caught with both hands in a cookie jar that didn't belong to him?

"Dad?" Now he was making me nervous. Really nervous. Like, was I going to have to kill him after all nervous.

"Fee." He ran one hand through his short hair

before exhaling heavily, shoulders slumping. "I wanted to tell you. I was going to, I swear. I just…"

Please don't be cheating. Please don't be cheating. Murder, mayhem, fine, I could live with that. But infidelity?

"Fee, I've been working." Um, holy, what? "For Clara. Since the show arrived." Working? Doing what? I must have blurted again because he answered that question next. "Investigating Ron Williams," he said. Dad looked about as guilty as I'd ever seen him, face turning red as he rushed on. "Fee, I got my private investigator license a month ago and I've been taking cases ever since."

CHAPTER TWENTY-NINE

He did not just drop a gigantic bombshell in my lap like that without any kind of warning whatsoever. "You *what*?" How had I not known he was thinking about this let alone gone ahead and took the plunge?

Dad seemed to regain some of his composure, though the almost giddy look of relief that crossed his face told me my reaction wasn't what he was expecting. "I've just been picking at it," he said. "You actually gave me the idea, and Crew pushed me to do it finally."

I knew the exact moment he was talking about, the push he mentioned. Had found it so strange at the time it happened, certainly didn't guess this was the reason for Dad's explosive anger. When Crew confronted Dad in his office and asked him if he was ready to take a badge, be a deputy again. I'd thought it was insult that drove my father from the sheriff's station, he was so pissed. But did Crew know what my father was contemplating, and did he purposely shove Dad into this idiotic idea he now grinned down at me about like he hadn't lost his damned fool mind?

If Crew knew—choke, *Daisy*. She knew, didn't she? They were both in so much trouble. But it explained why Dad suddenly had my back, encouraged me to investigate Sadie's death. He'd been contemplating his own exodus into extra-curricular busybody activities, clearly feeling guilty enough about it he'd stopped arguing the case for me to mind my own business. Dad was so far from it himself he had to have been hoping I'd agree to being an accomplice.

He must have finally registered I might not have initially blown my top over his reveal but was working my way up to handing him his butt on a plate because his grin faded, the happy little boy expression disappearing. While I struggled with needing to protect my mother who clearly had no idea because she'd have said something by now. And wanting my father to be happy, this happy, but did he have to do it behind my back?

"It's just been the odd case here and there," he said, like it was no big deal he'd started a company and was investigating crimes again but doing it in secret because he knew it was a terrible idea. Right, Fee, as terrible as me poking my nose around in police matters without even a PI license to back me up? Uh-huh, preach to the choir, sister. Besides, who said it was a bad idea?

"Dad." I blew out the breath I'd been holding and forced myself not to freak out. Wasn't my life, wasn't my choice. "Does Mom know?" Ah, there was the kicker, the moment of truth that really burned my socks. From his flinch of guilt, she had no freaking clue either. "Okay, so clearly you've lost your mind in your dotage and I'm going to have to have you committed." He scowled at me, but without any kind of weight behind it. "Seriously. You did this and didn't tell Mom. If I don't put you in a mental hospital, she'll realize you did this fully cognizant and kill you." I shook my head. "I won't be responsible for making myself half an orphan." If there was even such a thing. "Dad, Mom needs you right now. Way more than Clara Clark."

He looked agonized, the regret of it flickering over his face. "I know, Fee," he said. "But I agreed to this case before Ron died. I had no idea things were going to happen the way they did. I was already neck-deep and Clara kept calling."

I didn't have to say he could have quit the job. He didn't raise me to quit, either, but honestly. Then again, if it was me? Hell, I was standing here in this place right here and now because I couldn't mind my own business either.

Who was I to judge? I was his daughter, that's who.

"It was just meant to be backgrounds on

everyone, and some digging into Ron's cookbook. That's it." Dad dug his hands into the pockets of his ski jacket, misery descending. "I swear, it should have been quick and easy. Your mother would never have to know."

"You have to tell her, Dad." He did. He couldn't keep this from her.

"Fee, you can't say a word to Lucy." Was that panic on his face? Was my big, strapping, gun-toting former sheriff father afraid of my little mom? "Please, especially now. It'll break her heart."

Oh, so now he worried about that after the fact, huh? Typical. And I was just as bad, putting this murder ahead of my mother's state of mind.

Clara had the bad taste to reappear, joining us with a reluctant expression but more frustrated than anything. I glared to try to repel her but apparently, she was accustomed to being frowned at.

"John, we need to go." She nodded to me, more of a passing gesture at politeness.

"He's not going anywhere," I said. "You knew Ron Williams's cookbook was plagiarized and you didn't do a thing about it."

The shock on her face, on Dad's, was about as satisfying as it was telling.

"It what?" Clara looked like she was going to throw up.

"Gloria Kingsley," I said. And saw the understanding dawn across her expression in a rush of emotions from shock to horror to resignation.

"That bastard," she whispered. "He would have

ruined me."

"How so?" I glanced at Dad who didn't comment, his normal quiet focus returned.

"My name was on that book as an endorsement," she said. "If he went down, I'd be going with him. He did this on purpose."

"Because you were going to kick him off the show," Dad said.

Well now, that was a shift in perspective according to what she'd told me.

Clara's face scrunched. "That was supposed to be confidential, John."

"You said he told you he was getting his own show." What else had she lied about?

Clara huffed a sigh, tossed her hands. "I guess it doesn't matter anymore. Fine, I lied to you, John. It was the other way around. Ron was trying to leave me and without him, my show was over." She was on the verge of tears again.

"You realize I can't help you if you're going to keep things from me," Dad said, grim tone disappointed. Hey, he had it perfected, too, just like Crew. Must have been a cop thing.

"Who cares?" Her face puckered with the battle for control over her emotions. "He's dead, the book is a sham and I'm never going to get another show." Her voice climbed in volume and whininess until she shuddered and covered her face in her hands, crying again at last.

"Why were you with him the night he died?" I pushed her heartlessly and it worked.

"I told you," she said. "I was fighting with him about Janet. I didn't want her there. No one did. The cheating had to stop."

"But you bullied Molly to cheat," I said.

"It was all going to hell anyway." Clara pulled herself together with a visible shake and swallowed. "When I told him Molly said no, he dropped his exit on me, and that he was taking the book with him. Something about a producer wanting to turn it and him into his own series." So it wasn't just the publisher's advance luring him into moving ahead with the book? That offer had to have been why he'd risked publishing plagiarized material. He'd proven to me he wasn't forward-thinking enough to consider there might be consequences.

"What producer?" Did we have another suspect in play? If said producer found out about the copyright issues…

"Julian Parker," she said while I started in surprise. Wait, he was Willow Pink's manager. Since when did the arrogant ass dump his favorite starlet to be a producer? While we weren't besties or anything, I'd stayed in touch with the superstar. She hadn't mentioned anything about Julian leaving her. Was she behind this move? Maybe shifting out of acting on screen and to behind the scenes? At least I could check Julian off the suspect list. If he had shown his face in Reading again, I'd have recognized him immediately. "This is terrible," Clara interrupted my train of thought. "I need to call my agent."

"If your name is on the book," I said, "does that

mean you get a cut of the profits?"

Clara flinched, but she didn't cry again, angry this time. "Don't try to turn this on me," she said. "I get a cut, but it's a small percentage. The real beneficiary will be Bonnie."

"Did she know about the recipe theft?" I'd have to ask her, but it was worth prodding Clara.

"I have no idea," she snarled. Paused. "Molly's on the show. Gloria's granddaughter." Her eyes widened as she made the connection.

Ding, ding. Though I wasn't happy she'd made it, honestly. The fewer people who knew the better. "How much did she know about the cookbook?"

Clara shook her head, dazed now. How did she not have a migraine from crashing through emotion after emotion like that?

"Look," she said, "the show is done, and the book will either implode and burn or skyrocket, I don't care which. I'm over it." She glared at Dad. "You call yourself a detective. Your daughter knew more than you did. You're fired." She stomped away, muttering to herself, on her phone again as she left us there.

I turned to Dad, heart in my throat, but he didn't seem angry, more amused than anything.

"My kid," he said. "Way to one-up the old man, Fee. What else you got?"

No way was he getting out of the trouble he was in complimenting me. "Nice try," I said. "You have an appointment with your wife, Fleming. Now." He hesitated while I did my best not to drag him physically from the lobby. “Or I tell her for you.”

The unhappy look on his face as he sighed and nodded didn’t make me feel better. Not even a little bit.

CHAPTER THIRTY

I was never going to learn to mind my own business. Not even when it meant preventing hurting the people I loved the most in the world. I should have listened to Dad when he tried to reason with me all the way to his truck while I marched him to the door.

"This is terrible timing," he said. "It's not going to go well, Fee. Let me find the right time to tell her, please."

I should have stayed out of it, let him sort out how he was going to do the big reveal without sending Mom into a spiral. While my blood boiled with the need to drive him to his house myself to ensure he got there in one piece so Mom could take him apart personally for lying to both of us.

Yeah, should have just backed off and focused on murder.

Didn't.

Which meant, fifteen minutes after pulling out of the parking lot behind Dad's truck and following him all the way home in a rather self-righteous mood, I stood in their living room with my heart on the floor and my dad next to me with his head hanging. While my mother—my normally kind and thoughtful mother—shrieked at him at a volume and intensity that made it almost impossible to make out the individual words she was saying. Probably for the best because the few I did catch weren't nice at all and could be misconstrued as serious threats to his safety and cast doubt on his parentage.

Killing off any doubt I'd made a horrible, drastic and crippling mistake.

Dad took her audible assault for about a minute before he seemed to swell into this towering volcano of pending explosion and then he was shouting, too, his deep voice echoing through the house while Mom's counterpoint banshee wailing cut through my eardrums like a hot knife through butter.

I backed slowly away from the pair of them while they shouted profanities, accusations and the kinds of private things I really, really didn't need to know about their personal life, wishing I could take it all back. Just rewind time and not run into Dad at the Lodge, not let Mom enter the stupid damned TV show, protect her from Vivian's vitriol, just never come home to Reading after all.

Does it make me a coward I fled without trying to stop the fight? In all fairness, there wasn't anything I could do that wouldn't put me at risk of bodily harm. Okay, I'm going a bit far. I was about 99% positive Mom wouldn't hurt Dad and 100% the opposite, so it wasn't like they were going to really murder each other or anything. No, it wasn't their physical well-being at risk. I stood on the front porch a long moment, aching inside, kicking myself mentally over and over as the house echoed from the sound of their continuing fight.

I'd never, ever in all my years ever witnessed them argue. Yes, they discussed things and at times Mom could get cutting with words, Dad a bit harsh. But a fight? A real, honest-to-goodness shouting match of epic proportions, the likes of which carried on inside right now?

Never. And if someone told me they'd had this fight and I wasn't here to witness it? I'd have laughed in their face and told them to present video evidence, or it didn't happen.

I was so lost for what to do, how to help, I finally left, stumbling to my car, getting behind the wheel while tears trickled down my cold cheeks. I barely felt the chill in the air, registered I was driving before I found myself back on the highway to the Lodge, needing a distraction, anything to help me forget I may have just caused a giant rift between my parents.

No, wait. Not me. I would not claim this guilt as purely my own. I didn't sneak around behind Mom's back, lie to her, hide things from her. That was all

Dad. Still, there had to have been a better way to drop this on her than in the middle of her own identity crisis.

Way to go, Fee. Nice job.

My phone rang, the cheery sound making me feel ill. I answered hands-free, tapping the screen and letting it talk through my car speakers, barely registering who it was on the other end in my misery.

"Fee, it's Molly." She sounded nervous and when I finally paid attention, I remembered why I was going to the Lodge in the first place. The shadowy figure with their hands full of what I was pretty sure had to be gelatin-laced something for Janet's kitchen, sneaking on set just before Ron Williams was killed. "I need to see you. Can you meet me at the stage? I have something to show you."

"Is Crew there?" I wiped at the tears on my cheeks. At least I could get this right and not screw up his case.

"The sheriff?" She sounded confused. "No, I don't think so."

Damn, I must have missed him. Didn't matter. "I'll be there in about ten minutes."

"Thanks, Fee. See you soon."

Mom and Dad were on their own for now. I had a murderer to out.

I parked and was circling the building toward the back door when I hesitated, so focused on making this right I realized I probably should call Crew. But when I tried his number, it was busy. I left a hasty message as I entered the back door by the ski lift, not wanting to be seen entering the sound stage. I had something to check first before I talked to Molly, and I needed a moment of privacy to do it.

He'd just have to catch up with me.

The stage was quiet, empty. I circled around and checked the maintenance door again, found it clear, looking down the side of the construct to the front of the room where the camera took in the full space. The bulk of the front wall of the *Cake or Break* set cut off the view of the security feed into the murder scene, but, as the video Alicia shared proved, the line of sight to this door was free and clear. Some fingerprint powder and a comparison would reveal that my guess to the sneaking figure's identity was correct. Considering that person had no reason to use this particular exit paired with the video… looked like I had myself a murderer.

I hurried to the set kitchens, looking under the counters. I'd expected the contents to be gone, and I was right. That sent me into the green room area. My luck was with me, at least. The crew had packed everything into big plastic bins, each marked with the number of the kitchen set. Janet's had been #1, Molly's #2 and Mom's #3, before it became Joyce's. When I dug into the box I was looking for, I pulled out the dish and tasted the sugar.

That's all it was, just powdered sugar. Wasn't it? Right. Gelatin was odorless and tasteless. The only way to know for sure was to take it and test it. But maybe I was wrong, and the gelatin had been in the flour. Or something else in this kitchen was sabotaged. Janet wouldn't have made that accusation lightly, I was positive of it, and the gelatin made the most sense. What didn't was who I suspected of cheating. I guess because I just wanted to believe there was good in people after all.

Didn't change the fact someone was lying to me, and I had a few questions as to why.

I turned to the exit of the room, heading out into the halted deconstruction zone on the other side. I'd have this jar tested and tell Crew to bring the rest to the lab just in case. Head down, so focused on the container in my hands and what I thought it meant, I almost missed the scuff of feet nearby, the furtive movement of air close to me. I spun, too late, to the slow, silent collapse of the wall beside me as it crushed me under its weight and carried me to the floor.

CHAPTER THIRTY-ONE

I'd never really considered myself lucky per se, though I have been in quite a few scrapes along the way and typically come out the other side intact, or mostly intact. Case in point, as the wall fell, I acted on instinct and dove to the right, the canister still clutched against me. I aimed for a pile of stacked chairs that normally graced the dining room. I just managed to slide under them, head and shoulders protected, as the crashing set landed on my legs, pinning me a moment while I coughed from the dust raised by the collapse.

Panting and jerking on my boots that caught on the top edge, I finally wriggled my way out from under the stack, shaking from the adrenaline surge but happy to be intact. I'd be a bit bruised later, and likely sore in places I wasn't feeling yet past the rush of tingling that told me I was alive despite myself. At least this time I didn't end up with a concussion or in the hospital. I'd take it.

As I waved at the cloud of dust and gasped around particles trying to choke me, other hand in a death grip around the container of what I hoped was doctored sugar, I realized I wasn't alone. And froze, gaping, heart pounding, at the sight of Molly Abbott staring back at me from the other side of the fallen wall.

Right where someone would have to stand to push it over.

"Fee!" She lunged for me as I backpedaled from her, heading into the set proper, catching myself on the edge of the judge's table and using it to support me while I fumbled for my phone. Molly came to an abrupt halt, face already pale now peaking with pink on her cheeks, big eyes wide as she seemed to make some kind of mental connection. She whipped her head around, almost her whole upper body, before pivoting back, shaking her head, hands outstretched when I tried my best to scroll through my contacts and call Crew with fingers that wouldn't behave. "Fee, I didn't have anything to do with what just happened." I met her eyes, positive I couldn't trust her because I was an idiot and should have known all along she was a liar. Even now, authentic honesty shone through her worried expression, the way she leaned toward me but didn't try to approach. "Are you okay? Did you get hurt?"

I shook my head, hair whipping my cheek while I fought to speak, still holding my phone tight, the canister. "You tried to kill me." Hey, not the first person to give it a go and probably not the last if I was going to continue to push my luck. But seriously. I was so over it.

She shushed me softly like I was a terrified animal she needed to soothe. "It's okay, you're all right. Fee, I swear to you, I had nothing to do with it." She dropped her hands, tears in her eyes. "I came into the set to find you and heard something out back, so I went looking. I figured it was you. I was almost to the green room when I saw someone pass around the back of the set heading to the rear stairs. When I followed, they disappeared." She rubbed her upper arms with both hands in a brusque motion, nervously looking behind her again. "Could that have been the killer?"

I almost spoke before she closed the gap between us, now clearly afraid.

"Fee, I think I know who murdered Ron." She shivered as she whispered that in the now quiet of the set. No one had come to investigate the noise, so it must have been less of a bang outside the confines of the dining room than it felt when I'd been in the middle of it. I clutched my phone, wishing my fingers would stop shaking, as I nodded to Molly, chest tight with tension, my anger at my own gullibility came rushing back.

"So do I," I said. "And I'm looking right at her."

Molly gaped, fish lipping, shaking her head ever

so slightly, those points of pink on her cheeks now mottled patches climbing down her neck and under her collar. My fingers finally functioning, I pulled up the video Alicia sent me and stuck my phone in Molly's face, let her watch the evidence unfold, shaking the glass canister of sugar in my other hand while I spoke and she stared, guilt crawling over her features. Had I chosen the right ingredient to threaten her with? Didn't matter. It was pretty clear from her reaction I had her pegged.

"Yeah, that's right. You didn't know there was a camera that could pick up the maintenance stairs, did you? Well, there was. And it caught you coming back down to sabotage Janet." Every statement made her waver more, crushed her further but I was on a roll, and she wasn't getting away with this. Not any of it, including cheating. "You found Ron still here, probably gloating over his fight with Clara and you hit him over the head with the pot from Mom's box and then smothered him with the plastic bag to frame my mother."

Way to get myself worked up and ready to punch her in the face.

Molly's hands rose and covered her mouth, tears now free flowing down her cheeks, but she didn't argue so I knew I was right. I had her. And now that my fingers were working, I found Crew's number, hovered my thumb over dialing, even as Molly lunged for me and stopped me, misery in her eyes.

"I did it," she whispered. Flinched. "Not Ron. But Janet." She looked suddenly ill, a little green as she sagged, hand still tight on my wrist. "I cheated, Fee." Of course, she'd admit to the lesser accusation. Why then did it look like she wished she'd admitted to murder before coming clean about sabotage?

Damn it, compassion, take a hike.

"I couldn't stand it anymore." She released me, made no further effort to stop me from calling Crew while she sank to the stool that had been Ron's and sagged over the counter before her like a half-empty bag of flour. "She cheated and cheated and got away with it. And Clara supported it. I didn't know in the beginning, Fee, I swear. I wouldn't have been part of the show if I had known. It's not worth it to me." She held my gaze despite her guilt. What, to prove to me she was telling the truth? And I was falling for her story, wasn't I? Sigh. "When I found out I almost left the show, I told you that already. But Clara came to me, she told me the only way to save it was to cheat, to keep the ratings going. She said the fact I was in first place meant people already thought I was cheating." She snuffled, wiping at her cheeks with both hands. "I didn't know what to do, but I refused to go that far. Until this stupid special!" She wrung her hands before her then, fingers damp with tears. "If I hadn't had to bake against Janet, maybe I could have just let it go. But the way she treated Lucy, Fee. Your mother didn't deserve to be hurt that way. It wasn't her fault, and Janet needed to be taught a lesson."

"You knew they'd finish filming the show." I clenched the phone in my hand, Crew's number undialed, the canister of truth still between the two of us.

"Clara told us even before the sheriff came. She refused to stop. And I knew that meant Janet would be coming after me next."

"So, you decided to do something about it." I guess I understood that. But I'd have been more direct.

"I knew what she did from the taste I snuck of Lucy's cupcakes." Molly settled, no longer overly emotional but rather empty, deflated. "And I also knew I'd never get away with going as far as she did. I needed something to add to her mix she wouldn't taste in the batter, but that would ruin her bake in the oven."

"Gelatin." I was right. Wasn't I? "Am I right?"

She nodded. "How did you know?"

No way I was confessing the internet told me. "I guess I've picked up a thing or two." I sighed, relenting a bit myself. "That doesn't let you off the hook for Ron's murder."

Molly's distress returned. "I thought he was gone, that everyone had left," she said. "I didn't want witnesses, you should understand that." Fair enough, yes. She hesitated. Flinched. "I found the body before you did. He was already dead. But I didn't say anything to anyone because I knew how it would look."

"Because of the cookbook," I said.

Molly stilled, quieted. "What are you talking about?"

CHAPTER THIRTY-TWO

I'd had enough of her lying to me. "The cookbook, Molly. The one Ron was launching full of all the recipes your grandmother developed over her lifetime. The ones he stole from her when they were on the show together the first season. The same ones he was claiming were his own and planned to turn into a TV show." I scowled at her, made an ugly connection. "The reason you signed up for this circus in the first place."

For a moment I thought she was going to deny it. Lie again and ruin the small bit of credibility she'd built with me. Then, she shrugged, sad but not defiant. "I figured someone would make the connection eventually." Her little smile was weak. "Nice catch."

I didn't bother telling her it wasn't me, because Vivian wasn't getting any kudos for her part, thanks. Not even in the quiet of my mind. "So, it's true," I said. "You auditioned for the show because you found out he stole the recipes."

"No," she said. "But I knew about it after the fact."

Okay, I believed her when maybe I shouldn't have. "A coincidence?" Did that come out as heavily laced with disbelief as I aimed for?

She exhaled heavily. "Clara called me to audition. It was the tenth anniversary season and she wanted me on the show for the shock value. They were going to reveal my identity and the connection to my grandmother in the final episode." She stared down into her hands. "I almost said no. Grammy had terrible memories from her time with *Cake or Break*. But everyone encouraged me to do it, so I caved." She met my eyes again, so tired it showed in lines on her face, augmented by the dust my near-death raised to settle on her pale skin. "Ron gave me the creeps from day one, but he wouldn't leave me alone. I heard about the cookbook from him, the first time he hit on me. Like he didn't care he stole the recipes or that he was plagiarizing by publishing them."

"But you admit you knew prior to his death," I said in an ah-ha kind of tone because she just made my case for me despite the fact she immediately shook her head in denial. "You're telling me you didn't want to kill him for stealing your grandmother's recipes?"

"No," Molly said, swallowed. "Because while Ron stole them from Grammy, she wasn't innocent either."

She said what?

Molly's face pinched, her whole body shifting as she seemed to settle into resignation. "The recipes Grammy used on the first season of *Cake or Break* were already stolen," she said, "from her friends and other bakers she knew from the old country. People who didn't watch television and wouldn't say anything even if they did."

Yikes. Quite the legacy to follow up. Vivian wasn't going to like this one bit, was she? And why did I care how the Queen of Wheat felt about her idol's dark past? Well, I didn't.

Now, who was the liar?

"Grammy was as bad as Ron," Molly said, enough self-judgment in her voice I knew her whole angst over cheating to get back at Janet was deep-rooted in personal reasons that went beyond mere honesty and into what had to be a lifetime of swearing to never be her grandmother. "The collection of recipes she brought with her went missing the last night of the show, the night Ron sabotaged Grammy and took first place. She was furious, but there was nothing she could do. He found out about the thefts thanks to being a sneaking scumbag." She should talk, considering her grandmother was one, too, but that was for later. "He told her if she protested, he'd tell Clara the recipes weren't hers." So, Ron already knew? "When

I tried to tell him they were already stolen, wondering if Grammy lied about his threat, he laughed at me. Ron said he figured enough time had passed and he was famous enough he could do whatever he wanted." She bit her lower lip, glaring at me now, her anger the final piece I needed to accept her story. "Happy now?"

I wasn't and shook my head, so she'd see it. "Let's say I believe you," I said. "That doesn't mean you didn't kill him."

"I would have rathered he published," Molly said then, suddenly a hissing, furious bundle of revenge so startling I took a half step back. She pulled herself together, choking a moment and finally clearing her throat, fingernails digging into her thighs while she fought visibly for control. "I planned to win this show, Fee. To use my fame to expose him for a fraud and a thief. Take him down with his own arrogance. And if that meant my grandmother's name was besmirched, all the better."

"What did he do to you?" I almost hated to ask because that much vitriol hidden behind her innocent, kind mask? Couldn't be good.

"He assaulted me," she said, shaken but collected, "on several occasions. I always managed to escape. I tried to turn him in to Clara the first time, but she wouldn't listen." My disgust meter skyrocketed. "That day, the day he died, he grabbed me, kissed me before I could stop him. Oh, I *wanted* to kill him. But I didn't." She sniffed, stiffening with her jaw set. "No, I'm not sorry he's dead. Still, there's a part of me that would have rathered see him suffer."

Revenge I bought hook line and sinker, to the point I set the canister down on the counter between us and reached forward toward her. Molly flinched like I threatened her then sobbed once when she realized I was offering support. Probably the first show of anything of the kind since she joined this wretched show, poor thing. Sheesh, I was such a sucker. But if showing compassion to someone meant I had softhearted issues, so be it.

She grasped my hand tightly in hers, lips twitching before she was able to speak. "I know I'm a terrible person who would have made sure his reputation was burned to the ground," she said. "But I had no reason to kill him. I'm not a murderer."

Likely I'd lost my mind in the last few minutes, but I believed her. "Did you see anyone else on the set when you were planting the tainted sugar? Or do you know of anyone who had a reason to kill Ron?"

Molly hesitated then, biting her lower lip, tears returning. She gestured at my phone and I handed it over. Watched her close the call screen and bring up the video again before turning it toward me.

"The person who showed me that way onto the set," she said, "the same person who promised me there wasn't a camera watching it and who made sure I could get on and off without anyone seeing me just in case I needed a way to escape Ron."

"Who?" I met her eyes as a voice interrupted, soft and low.

"I guess that would be me."

CHAPTER THIRTY-THREE

I spun, gasping in fright, memory of the falling wall and being struck on the back of the head so hard I passed out flashing through my mind. I ducked as I turned on impulse, though I must have looked ridiculous, because the person standing behind me, watching Molly with haunted, sorrow-filled eyes, wasn't lunging for me. Though the gun he held in his hand wasn't exactly a kindly offer to come quietly.

Dale only had eyes for Molly, ignoring me while I slipped with the kind of baby deer awkwardness I seemed to default to, grasping at the counter and using it as a lifeline while the pair stared at each other as if I didn't exist.

"Dale." Molly breathed his name, real regret in her voice. "What did you do?"

"I couldn't take it," he said, anguished, love-struck, so broken in those brief words my heart hurt for him despite the gun pointed in my general direction. "He was evil, Molly, cared nothing for anyone but himself." Tears trickled down his cheeks though his gun never wavered. "I saw him beat down and conquer so many women in the last four seasons I worked for this show, it disgusted me. And Clara wouldn't do anything to stop him." The softness of his despair hardened as he spoke her name. "I was furious that night, about Janet's cheating, about Clara's attitude, but mostly about Ron. Molly," he whispered her name. "I love you. I just couldn't live with it anymore."

She sighed out her sorrow in a screen-worthy release of air. "Dale, I love you, too." She pattered her hands in her lap as if wishing she could rush to him but unable to make herself move further than that tiny effort.

Dale shook his head then, turning his face away, jaw tight. "You told me you were afraid of him. I showed you that side exit so you could escape him, not go to him. But I saw you alone with him." His voice shook. "I saw you kiss him, how you embraced him. You said you cared about me, but you were just like all the others."

Okay, I'd expected a more jaded outcome, not some saga of emotional angst. What was I supposed to do to get the gun away from someone with a broken heart?

"What you saw was Ron taking what he couldn't

get by consent," Molly said, so much power behind her tone Dale's head whipped around. "How many times did I have to tell you? I despised him, Dale."

"I heard him tell Clara he had you in his pocket," Dale said, breathless now. "That he talked you into cheating and that you agreed to support the cookbook."

A flare of anger crossed her face. "He lied," she said, blunt, plain. "And you believed him?"

Dale wavered, the gun wobbling in his hand. I felt like I was in the middle of a soap opera, and it wasn't going to end with hugs and kisses and riding into the sunset. The way he was going, it was more likely wrapping up with two dead chicks and a pretty boy suicide. But I stood frozen, indecisive, my phone too far to reach on the counter between Molly and me while the drama unfolded without me.

Enough of things happening outside my control. "You killed Ron for Molly." And I had to draw attention to myself, right?

But Dale didn't seem to care about me at that moment. Instead, he addressed his next words to Molly. "I waited until you and Clara left and confronted him. I just wanted to know the truth, to hear it from his lips. Tell him to leave you alone once and for all." He choked on a bark of a laugh. "You know, he didn't even know my name? I've worked with this show for four years," his gun hand accentuated the time frame with little jerks that ratcheted my anxiety by about a billion degrees, "and he didn't know my name."

"He wasn't worthy of your name," Molly whispered.

Dale hesitated, stilled, then went on, finally meeting my eyes with his dull ones, choosing that moment to remember I was there. Awesome. "I didn't mean to. I didn't confront him to kill him. Things just got out of hand." He sounded so young and vulnerable, free hand rising to shakily wipe at his forehead, a gleam of sweat on his skin shining in the emergency lights over the set. "How did they get so out of hand?" His eyes met mine. "I didn't take your mother's pot on purpose. It was just closest. And the plastic bag in the trash… all a coincidence. I swear it, Fee. I never tried to implicate Lucy."

Well, he had that going for him in my books. Not much more, though. "Didn't stop you from trying to kill me, though, did it?"

Dale wavered. "I was scared. I knew you were onto me. Or thought you were. I never wanted to hurt anyone." He blinked, trembled. "I just wanted to keep Molly safe."

The focus of his attention rose from her seat, crossed in front of the counter. I reached for her, to stop her, but she shook her head at me, sad smile small and tender.

"I came back," she said. "To plant the gelatin in Janet's kitchen."

He nodded in clear misery. "I was here. I saw you do it." His whole body trembled. "It's okay, Molly. I get it, you had to."

"I didn't," she said, crying herself all over again.

"I could have quit the show. But then I thought I'd never see you again."

And then they were crying together, her standing in front of him, the gun forgotten between them, and I almost had a heart attack from the tension of it all.

"I didn't want you to know what I did." Her wail of despair matched his like sabotage and cheating were as bad as murder.

He nodded then. "I didn't judge you, not for a second." Dale's own small smile was full of love. "Not one, Moll."

They wavered there, hearts clearly linked, my own struggling to pump enough oxygen into my brain so I didn't pass out.

"It was a crime of passion, Dale," I said, trying to keep my voice low and reasonable despite the thickness of the air that I swore could be cut with a knife. I'd heard that expression used before, but I'd never felt it until now. Felt oddly appropriate. "A jury will understand that. Please, just put the gun down and let's talk to the authorities."

He snapped it around to point at me, ignoring the fact Molly stood next to him. "I can't," he said. "Don't you see? I killed Ron and I'll go to jail. I'll lose Molly forever."

For a brief, terrifying moment I was positive he was going to pull the trigger. The way her expression flickered, it seemed Molly was on his side, too. She would let him shoot me, the two star-crossed lovers ready to murder me and escape together and no one would ever know.

Clearly, I'd been watching too many movies. And totally misjudged Molly. Instead of turning to join him, she very gently touched his wrist, the one holding the gun at me, and smiled a wavering, brave smile.

"You can't lose me," she said, blinking through her tears. "I'm not going anywhere."

That's how I found myself making a shaking, hasty call to Crew with a gun sitting on the counter in front of me while Molly and Dale hugged each other and whispered their love for one another while I did my best not to burst into hysterical giggles at how utterly screwed up the world was.

CHAPTER THIRTY-FOUR

I wasn't expecting his visit, but when Crew showed up at the door of Petunia's that night, I let him in without a word, not even thinking about it when I led him downstairs to my apartment before stopping to consider what doing so might imply.

Blushing.

He didn't comment on our location, though, crouching to scratch Petunia's ears while he spoke.

"I wanted to check on you," he said, "after today's excitement."

Crew had been oddly kind and rather sweet to me when he'd come to my aid, answering the call almost immediately, already on his way when I finally managed to dial his number. I'd heard the siren in the background, realized he'd gotten my earlier message and was riding to the rescue.

A bit late, but when he listened to me unfold the story while Jill watched over the lovers—the pair ignoring her in favor of hugging each other and continuing to whisper sweet nothings like Dale hadn't murdered for Molly's honor—he didn't yell at me or even seem angry. Instead, to my shock, he held very still a long moment when I rambled to a halt before stepping in and embracing me for a brief, glorious instant of awesome.

"I'm glad you're okay," he said, low and gruff, before letting me go. I'd stood there for the longest time while he asked Dale a few questions, had Jill gently cuff him and lead him away, after bagging the gun on the counter.

Hard to believe that had been a few hours ago and not a lifetime. I leaned back against the counter in my kitchen, not sure what to say.

"Thank you for checking in on me," I finally managed as he straightened from his attentions to my pug, much to her disappointment. She sat herself firmly on his feet and stared up at him in clear adoration while he spoke.

"I just wanted to be sure you weren't hurt." He flushed a bit. "After what happened in April, I mean. The concussion and everything. You're sure you're okay?" He knew about the wall falling on me.

"I guess I'm luckier than the average redhead," I said.

Crew's flash of a smile died as he stood there, hands diving into his back pockets. For once, he was the awkward one, shifting from one foot to the other, disturbing Petunia who simply muttered and moved herself over to reclaim his boots for her butt.

"Fee." He coughed softly, looked down at the pug using him for a sofa. "About the other night."

He couldn't have crushed me more thoroughly than he did with the weight of those four words.

"It's okay," I said, choking on trying to be a grownup when he obviously was here to tell me it had been a mistake, kissing me like that. "You don't have to say anything." I was such an idiot. Did I really think he was into me?

Crew frowned, meeting my eyes, his tightening around the edges. "I don't think you understand," he said. Before closing the distance between us with two long strides and kissing me all over again.

Kissing Crew would never get old.

His lips parted from mine after a brief, passionate moment that was gone way too soon. "I owe you an apology," he said, gruff and deep. "I've left you hanging for months, not sure how to approach this."

"You're doing just fine now," I whispered back. "More of this works great."

He chuckled over my mouth, hands on my hips, his body pressing me gently into the counter behind me. Just enough weight I knew he was there, felt his warmth without being uncomfortably squished.

"Good to know," he said. Sighed. "Oh, Fee."

"Oh, Crew." I let my hands rise, run around his waist to clasp behind him so he knew without a doubt I wasn't backing down. "Just say it and we'll sort it out. I think we've head-butted enough that if we're still standing here like this we'll survive anything you might fumble over."

His eyes twinkled, lips turning into a smirk. "Thanks."

"You're welcome." I stared at his mouth for so long I felt myself leaning in to kiss him again before I forced my eyes upward to his blue ones. "I can take it, Crew. Just say what you need to and let's figure this out if we can."

"I've never met anyone who infuriates and frustrates and makes me as crazy as you do." He laughed to take the edge off, leaning his forehead against mine. I wasn't insulted. Because I totally understood, and the feeling was rather mutual. Maybe not the best basis for a relationship? "Or someone who makes me laugh and want to protect her while being so proud of how amazing she is." Okay, that was better.

"But." I pushed him back just a bit, so I could focus because it was clear from the weight of his voice this was important.

"No buts," he said. "I've been using the excuse that this town has your back and not mine when that's not fair to you." I had no idea what he meant, but he wasn't done so I let him go on, partly because I needed to hear what he had to say. "Your interfering with my cases was the perfect excuse to keep you at arm's length. All I did was make us both miserable." I wanted to hug him, to tell him it was all right, but he wasn't done. "I'm not here to ask you to forgive me for being a jackass," he said. "I'm here to ask you for a bit more patience if you're willing to wait for me. To let her go."

Let her…

Choke.

"Your wife." I swallowed hard past the knot in my throat. "Crew, I'd never ask you to do that."

He shook his head, hugged me then, tucking me under his chin, the fabric of his coat crinkling beneath my hands as I embraced him back.

"She'd be pissed at me, Fee," he whispered in a thick voice. "For hanging onto her for so long. She wanted me to be happy, made me promise to find someone else. I said I would, but I didn't mean it. And then I met you and I had to face the fact Michelle was right. I had to find a way to move on."

So much hurt, more so than when we'd talked in April. "I don't want to be the cause of your pain." Too late for that, I guess.

"You're not." He gently released me, smiled down at me, blue eyes bright. "I am. I'm a stubborn idiot and a bit slow on the uptake. But if you're willing to be patient just a little bit longer…" He kissed me again, this time slow and soft and gentle until I wanted to melt into a puddle at his feet. Was surprised when his lips left mine I hadn't done so already. "It's going to be so easy to fall in love with you," he said, "but I don't want Michelle's memory between us when I do."

I wasn't sure that was going to be possible, but it wasn't my heart that had been broken by her death.

"I don't mean I'm going to forget her," he said, catching my hands with his. "Just that you deserve my whole heart. If that's something you want."

I could only think of one way to answer him. When he kissed me back, I knew he took my reply as the resounding yes I meant it to be.

CHAPTER THIRTY-FIVE

From the anxious expression on Aundrea's face and how Pamela's hand patted her fiancé's gently in a steady, soothing beat I knew they'd been talking to Mom even before the former spoke.

"Are you sure everything is still going ahead for the wedding?" They'd barely sat down at my kitchen counter five seconds ago, Daisy taking their coats, the pair not even looking at the coffee I set in front of them.

"I'm positive," I said, doing my best to exude confidence with a broad smile while I hoped I didn't just lie to my friends. "Everything's fine, just a few hiccups. To be expected, right?" I sipped my own mug of java as I sat and pushed the plate of sugar cookies toward them. "Snack?"

Pamela took one while Aundrea's hands settled in her lap, clutching at each other as if she needed the support.

"Your mother sounded like she really meant it," Aundrea said, glancing at Pamela who sighed and shrugged before meeting my eyes.

"We're still getting married," the newspaperwoman said, practical as ever, "in the annex. I'm sure if Lucy can't do the cake, Fee will take care of everything. Right, Fee?" Was that pleading for backup in her gaze?

"Of course," I said, wingwomaning like mad. "You have nothing to worry about, Aundrea. We're so excited to host the wedding. It's going to be gorgeous."

"I know." She seemed to relent, a flash of an excited smile crossing her lovely face. Jared definitely took after his beautiful mother, lucky him. "It's just we've waited so long. I want everything to be perfect."

The worry that I'd taken on Bridezilla wasn't lost on me, but they were my friends and I trusted Pamela to make sure her true love didn't give me an ulcer between now and May.

"Fee," Daisy said with a smile, "maybe Aundrea would like to see the new dining room in the annex? And the flooring Alicia picked out?" She gushed over the couple with the perfect amount of charm and charisma. "Stunning. Your photos are going to be epic."

Aundrea rose immediately and went with my

bestie, but Pamela lingered, her shrewd expression as she narrowed her eyes, grinning, telling me she'd hoped to get me alone.

"Tell me everything," she said, no-nonsense journalist shining through. "I can't believe I let Aundrea take me away for the weekend and I missed the story of the year."

"Well," I said, "of the month, anyway." Wrinkled my nose and sighed over my cup.

She laughed, patted my hand much as she had her fiancé's. "You'll feel better if you tell me everything. Just us friends."

My turn to laugh. "No, you'll have a scoop for the *Gazette*. But what are friends for?"

By the time Aundrea and Daisy returned, the pair chattering their excitement over the progress of the annex and my best friend's event plans, the beaming bride-to-be seemed soothed past her jitters and worries while Pamela shot me a wry grin as I wrapped up the story.

I hugged them both before Daisy guided them out, Pamela pausing at the kitchen door with one eyebrow arched.

"You think any more about that column we talked about?" She straightened her coat, shoulders shrugging to settle the fabric, gaze level but amused. "Since you're not showing any sign of keeping your nose clean?"

"Still thinking about it," I said. Blushed. Hated that I blushed. She laughed and I waved her off, turning to clean up the coffee cups as she left, the sound of Daisy seeing them off muffled when the kitchen door swung closed.

I had to go see Mom and talk some sense into her, not that I hadn't tried. Oh, I'd tried. Daisy tried. Wasn't doing much good, but I refused to quit on my mother. Didn't help she and Dad were still fighting, though it seemed the yelling, screaming and throwing things—if the big chunk of drywall missing from the living room and the vanished lamp by the fireplace was any indication—was over, their cold distance wasn't lost on me when I went to visit them after walking away from almost being shot again.

I hadn't meant to dump what happened on them. I'd just gone to see them, to check on them and ended up spilling the rest of the story while Dad frowned, silent, and Mom trembled, face tight with anger.

Wasn't expecting her reaction. "You see, Fiona? You see what poking your nose in gets you? If you get shot next time, don't come crying to me!" And then she stomped from the room and slammed her door while Dad refused to meet my eyes.

It had only been a day since, but I was pretty sure time wasn't the solution to this problem. Mom's reaction might have hurt at the moment, but I knew better. She wasn't mad at me. And from the conversation we'd had at the annex, she wasn't really mad at Dad, either. The Mom I loved wouldn't stay mad if he was truly happy doing what he was doing.

So, what would it take to heal her heart? I wished I knew. I hated seeing my normally loving parents divided, no matter what the cause. It wasn't like them and gave me an unsettled and uncomfortable fear to linger over.

At least someone got a reasonably happy ending over this. Bonnie and Joyce departed this morning, the best of friends, already in talks with Julian Parker about an investigative cooking show to uncover stolen recipes. Seriously, how ironic could you get? And shortly after they'd departed? I'd gotten a call from Molly. Dale was going to plead guilty in exchange for a plea bargain and she'd been offered her own show, courtesy of Clara.

Janet was the only one who'd ended up with the short end of the shortbread cookie. From what I heard she'd slunk out of town with her tail between her legs. Hopefully, that was the last I'd hear from her. Surely, she was done, exposed as a cheater? Just her luck, she'd end up with her own show, too. Not likely, but the world was a weird, weird place.

I shook my head to myself as I put the mugs in the dishwasher, turning to smile at Daisy who returned, Petunia trailing after her.

The pug hurried to my side when she saw the dishwasher open, the disappointment on her face no crumbs escaped its confines during my task making me grin.

"What are we going to do about your mother?" Daisy sank to the stool Pamela vacated.

"Maybe I should tell her Vivian's making the cake," I said. "That might snap her out of it." Or make things worse. I still hadn't decided if I was going to tell my blonde rival about Gloria Kingsley's fraud or not. There was a time I would have rubbed it in her face just to piss her off. Maybe I really was growing up because there had been enough hurt passed around lately.

Daisy picked at a sugar cookie, absently offering Petunia a piece before wincing and wrinkling her nose at me. "Sorry."

Uh-huh. I sat next to her, taking the rest of the cookie she'd been massacring.

"Oh!" Daisy perked. "You said you wanted to tell me something and to remind you about it."

I did? For a long moment, I frowned, trying to think. It had been a pretty busy few days, what with the murder and Mom and Dad and Crew kissing me—

I could tell from the shocked look on Daisy's face I was blushing hard enough it surprised her. She grasped my hand, leaning close, eyes huge.

"What?"

I coughed on a crumb of cookie before a goofy smile won. Daisy prodded me and I realized I'd been lost in the memory. I inhaled, flashed her a smile filled with hope and broke a cookie in half.

"Crew kissed me." Was giggling appropriate? Because I couldn't help it. "Twice." Or was it three times? Did multiple kisses in two instances warrant multiple kissing claims? I'd leave the details to mystery.

Daisy's face lit up and she clapped like a little girl in excitement before hugging me hard, knocking part of my cookie on the floor. And that made Petunia happy, so it was all good.

I spent the next few minutes gushing over him and our possible future at her insistence. When I was finally done, Daisy sighed, resting her chin on her hand, dreamy look on her face.

"Well, finally," she said. Perked. "Or almost finally? No first date yet?"

I was not going to let myself retreat from excited to worried. That was something that could wait until he was ready. I wasn't in a hurry anymore or doubting. He'd made it clear enough he cared, hadn't he? And that he was putting my happiness first, ahead of rushing into something before he could give me his full attention. So whatever happened now, I was done worrying about Crew Turner.

At least about his heart. Did I need to be concerned about how he seemed to think this town had it in for him because of Dad and me? Let Olivia just try to fire him or whatever was going on with town council now that I was this close to a date. We'd see who lost their job, wouldn't we?

Daisy hesitated and I almost groaned. Was she going to give me a hard time? Force the issue? Well, maybe she was right, and I should march over to his house and see if he was home. If he had beer. If his lips still tasted so good—

I jerked out of my reverie when her face fell and she squared her shoulders, turning to the big purse she'd abandoned on the next stool over shortly after arriving this morning. She fished out a stack of familiar-looking envelopes, clutching them tightly before setting them in front of me with a forced smile. I knew them immediately, of course. The letters Daniel Munroe wrote to Grandmother Iris, the same ones I found in my back yard a year and a half ago, buried in a metal box in a flower bed. Pete's death came rushing back, along with the memory of Peggy and my first near-death experience when Daisy spoke.

"Sorry to have these so long," she said, a bit breathless.

"No name ideas?" I frowned down at the letters, wondering why they'd upset Daisy.

"No," she said. Tsked softly. "And no treasure. I don't think." More hesitation, enough to make me head tilt.

"What's up, Day?" She seemed flustered, almost embarrassed. Well, from the few lines I'd read of a couple of the letters, they'd been pretty intimate. But Daisy wasn't usually such a prude. That was my department.

She blew out her full lower lip in a gust of air. "Thing is, I was sure I found something, but I couldn't have because I'm not smart like you are." I gaped at her while she flapped her hands at me, nostrils flaring as she tossed her dark blonde hair like she'd said too much. "Everyone knows I'm dumb." Her little laugh came out brittle. "I just thought maybe I could find something about the treasure, you know? And I thought I did but I couldn't have so let's just drop it."

I'd never known my bestie to ramble and I was so shocked by her self-assessment and following diatribe of Daisydowner, I almost didn't catch her in time as she lurched to her feet, clearly trying to escape before she could say anymore. But I moved without thinking, the one time it really paid off to have good reflexes, and grabbed her, dragging her down again to the stool while I scowled at her with my best Lucy Fleming face.

"My darling Daisy," I said. "Don't you ever, ever talk about yourself like that in front of me again. No, correct that." I snapped my fingers in her face. "In the privacy of your own ridiculous head, either. Hear me, missy?"

She blinked at me through her lashes. "You're always so nice to me." Was that a hitch in her voice? "You don't have to be, you know. I'm fine with not being smart."

"Daisy," I said, pouring all of my sincerity and everything in my heart into the next few words, "I'm not being nice. I'm being honest. You're not dumb. And anyone who thinks you are can suck it. Okay?"

She giggled faintly. Relaxed. "Okay," she whispered. "Thanks, Fee."

"That's better." I grabbed the letters and shook them at her. "Now, show me what you found before I smack you with these."

She took them with trembling hands, sorted the envelopes as she spoke. "It's not the letters," she said. "I read them all before I realized that." She blushed again, sparkling laugh delightful. "Your grandmother, Fee. I had no idea Iris was so passionate." She fanned herself with a breathless laugh before her hands returned to their work. I watched as she shifted the envelopes around, eyes widening when a pattern fell into place, familiar as my own face when she finished. "The message wasn't inside."

It was outside. Clear as day—no pun intended—when they were all laid out together.

I'd noticed the pen strokes on the edges of the paper, but I'd thought they were all mistakes or slips of the nib. Inconsequential to the contents of the letters themselves. But when Daisy made a flower shape with the envelopes, layering them together into the rough shape of an iris—no, the symbolism was not lost on me—I realized the lines that looked abstract made up a symbol. One I knew very well and that sent shivers through me.

The off-center compass from the scrap of the map in my music box stared back at me. Along with a single word.

"Markham." Daisy said it out loud while I gaped. "I looked it up. Fee, there was a historian who wrote a book about the Reading treasure. And his last name was—"

"Markham!" I lunged for her and hugged her. "Daisy! You're brilliant."

She beamed at me. I think it could have ended right then and there, in fact, and I'd have done a solid for my bestie she'd carry with her for the rest of her life. But this was far from over. I leaped up, grabbing her coat and tossing it to her, reaching for Petunia's harness.

Daisy watched me with huge eyes and a grin on her face as I grabbed my own puffy coat from the kitchen door hook, hopping into my boots while she laughed.

"Where are you going?" She slipped on her own jacket when I tucked the fat pug into her boots.

"The library, Day," I said. Paused. "Unless you've already been there?"

She ducked her head. Reached for her purse. "I wanted to wait for you."

Of course, she did.

CHAPTER THIRTY-SIX

We bounced out the front door of Petunia's, pug in tow, laughing and talking all the way to the center of town and the library there. All hail the conquering heroettes and all that. It was the kind of perfect crystal cold day January winters in these parts were famous for, the wind brisk enough I felt it but didn't care, not while Daisy hurried along beside me, Petunia barking her happiness at being outdoors and our delighted, excited state. I even swung my arms in unbridled joy, embracing the moment of adventure, skipping a few steps to the sound of Daisy's laughter.

It wasn't about finding the treasure on that sunny winter afternoon. Sure, finding it would be amazing, over the top awesomesauce with a dose of holy Hannah thrown in for good measure. If I thought

Petunia's was busy now… never mind the fact-finding the hoard would mean I'd never have to actually work again if I didn't want to. I'd never dreamed of being stinking rich, but the idea appealed, nonetheless.

No, that half skip, bubbling walk of joy was about being with Daisy, about feeling happier than I had in a long time, having a good laugh when the blues and loneliness tried for so long to win but failed miserably in the face of friendship and the hunt for pirate gold.

It was a beautiful day in Reading, Vermont.

When we reached the statue of our town's namesake, I stopped, uncontrollable giggling taking me over before I saluted him, Daisy bouncing on her toes as she snorted over my gesture and pointed at the front of his bronze pants glittering with more than frost clinging to the metal. Someone had been regularly defacing the poor guy and today was no different, a terribly graphic phallic symbol spray-painted across the front of his breeches. I found the fact oddly hilarious as we continued on, snorting into the cold air long after we passed him, all the way up the steps we ran two at a time to the door to the library.

There was a great deal too much giggling and whispering and carrying on happening between Daisy and me for Mr. Lightmews's liking, apparently, because we got the librarian death glare the moment we entered. I felt like a bad kid set loose in a candy store with intent to wreak havoc and didn't care,

Daisy hurrying me past the huffing older gentleman, Petunia trotting gamely between us. I was pretty sure dogs weren't allowed and that we had about a minute of hunting to find the book in question before Mr. Lightmews did his best to kick our overly excited butts out, but it would be enough.

I'd already gotten so much out of the last few minutes to keep me running on happy for a lifetime. Finding the treasure? Icing on this particularly tasty cake.

Heh. You'd think I'd have had enough of baking metaphors by now.

When I steered us toward the file catalog, Daisy grasped my arm firmly and jerked me toward the steps to the second floor.

"I already know where it is," she whispered so loudly it echoed. Good thing we were alone in here, then, at least from what I could tell. More giggling. Awesome. My cheeks already ached from grinning so hard I was sure my face was frozen that way. I followed her in a rush, scooting down a line of shelves until she stopped abruptly, making me bump into her and snort over the impact. She flapped her hands at me, shushing me loudly enough to be heard in the next town over, pulling me to a halt next to her while I snickered over anticipation of Mr. Lightmews's imminent command to depart or else. The most fun ever.

Daisy met my eyes before nodding to the shelf and the spine of a book right in front of me. I turned to her then, open-mouthed and wanting to smack her as I realized not only did she know where the book was theoretically, she'd scouted its exact location and had the restraint to do nothing about it. I could only wish for that kind of self-control.

"Why didn't you look?" I reached for the thin spine and pulled it down, plastic covering the paper flaps crinkling in my hands. The image of a huge ship and a treasure chest layered over top framed by the name Alistair Markham and the title, *The Reading Hoard: Fact or Fiction.*

She was still grinning, but now tears lined her big eyes as she blinked too fast. There was hurt behind her happy. I'd have to do something about that. "I wasn't sure, and I didn't have the courage to check myself." She squeezed my arm, grinned then, laughed out the last of her tension. "I'm an idiot. But I wanted you to be here anyway."

I winked at her, grasped the front cover. "Ready to find the treasure of Captain Reading, matey?" My pirate lingo was passing at best, but Daisy saluted anyway, much as I had the statue whose fortune we pursued.

"When you are, cap'n," she said.

Treasure or no treasure, wild goose chase or end of the road, whatever this book and the clues my grandmother left me meant?

I'd take all the fun I could get.

The Reading Reader Gazette

VOLUME 1 ISSUE 1 | JANUARY 11TH, 2019 | WWW.RRGAZETTE.COM

News Briefs

1. **Sidewalk Farmer's Market:** Town council has approved a street side farmer's market from June until September of this year. Anyone interested in renting a space for said market should get in touch with Susan at the mayor's office before March 1st.

2. **Parking Violations:** Your town council would like to remind you that parking restrictions are ongoing this winter. Due to increased snowfall and tourist activity, a year-round ban on street parking will be firmly enforced. Any Reading resident whose vehicle is found parked outside their driveway or on town property, taking up valuable parking space for visitors and in the way of our hard-working plow drivers, will be towed at their expense. Let's keep Reading's streets safe!

3. **Dog Waste Issue:** It has come to the attention of council that there's been an increase in dog waste appearing on our sidewalks. While maintenance staff is working hard to remove the problem, it's up to individual Reading residents to police their pooch's output! Fines will be levied by the sheriff's department for all infractions. Scoop your poop, please!

4. **Vandalism Continues:** While likely amusing to whoever insists on defacing the statue of our town founder, would whoever the budding artist is please refrain from phallic symbols and other content of a sexual nature. Thank you!

Winner of this week's Fire Hall 50/50 draw: Mandy Sterling. Congratulations, Mandy!

Please send any pending community notices to: pamela@rrgazette.com before 4PM.

The Reality of Murder

Dale Lewis, 24, of Fairmont, CA, is in custody for the murder of reality baking show Cake or Bake's Ron Williams

Love can be murder when bakers turn up the cheat

By Pamela Shard

In a rage fed by jealousy and unrequited love, Dale Lewis, 24, production assistant for the visiting reality show, *Cake or Bake*, struck famed baking show judge Ronald Williams, 62, with a pot from the set before smothering him with a plastic bag and leaving his dead body to be discovered by our very own Fiona Fleming.

In a scandal of cheating, unwanted advances and a plagiarized cookbook, Williams's death is shrouded in enough controversy the long-lived Cake or Bake reality show has been officially cancelled due to the loss of its most famous judge, according to show creator Clara Clark.

"I'm devastated by the loss," Ms. Clark said. "Ron's and my show's."

According to sources, Mr. Lewis's motive for murder had a heartfelt defense. In a misguided attempt to shield this year's rising star, Molly Abbott, Mr. Lewis's temper got the better of ended the life of Mr. Williams in an attempt to keep Ms. Abbott from unwanted attentions. The alleged mix of unreported assault, infidelity, cheating by last year's winner as well as reports that Mr. Williams's soon-to-be released cookbook, *Cake or Break Bread* is, in fact, a collection of stolen recipes he'd taken from Ms. Abbott's deceased grandmother, unravelled the popular show until murder, it seems, was inevitable.

Mr. Williams's widow, Bonnie Williams, vows to carry on in the industry despite her loss. "Ron would want me to succeed," she told this reporter. "My new business partner and I are launching a brand new show, to dig into the dirty underbelly of the cooking world."

Sheriff Crew Turner acknowledged the assistance of Fiona Fleming in solving this crime, putting her life at risk yet again for Reading.

May it be noted this is yet another in a string of murders that have ravaged Reading since the influx of tourism Mayor Olivia Walker

Looking for more Fiona Fleming? Have no fear, book six is available now! Find ***Ropes and Trees and Murder*** at your favorite retailer!

AUTHOR NOTES

My darling reader:

I'm a terrible cook and an even worse baker, but I adore cooking shows and watch them until I lie to myself I'm actually decent at anything to do with the culinary arts. My family's patience when I think—after several episodes of *You Gotta Eat Here* or *Beat Bobby Flay*—I can actually make food without a recipe is legendary.

Didn't stop me from wanting to dive into the world Lucy Fleming loves. Not just out of a misguided adoration for the food world I'll never be able to bring justice to. I've been having so much fun tapping into the different people in Fee's world, drawing out their strengths and weaknesses, finding out just how human and real and flawed they are that doing so is my temptation to create.

Exploring Reading's residents has been as satisfying for me as a delicious bite of the most extraordinary chocolate cake.

Rich. Velvety. Fulfilling. With more servings to come.

I hope you found this latest murder as delicious as I did.

Best,

Patti

ABOUT THE AUTHOR

EVERYTHING YOU NEED TO know about me is in this one statement: I've wanted to be a writer since I was a little girl, and now I'm doing it. How cool is that, being able to follow your dream and make it reality? I've tried everything from university to college, graduating the second with a journalism diploma (I sucked at telling real stories), am an enthusiastic member of an all-girl improv troupe (if you've never tried it, I highly recommend making things up as you go along as often as possible) and I get to teach and perform with an amazing group of women I adore. I've even been in a Celtic girl band (some of our stuff is on YouTube!) and was an independent film maker (go check out the Lovely Witches Club at www.lovelywitchesclub.com). My life has been one creative thing after another—all leading me here, to writing books for a living.

Now with multiple series in happy publication, I live on beautiful and magical Prince Edward Island (I know you've heard of Anne of Green Gables) with my multitude of pets.

I love-love-love hearing from you! You can reach me (and I promise I'll message back) at patti@pattilarsen.com. And if you're eager for your next dose of Patti Larsen books (usually about one release a month) come join my mailing list! All the best up and coming, giveaways, contests and, of course, my observations on the world (aren't you just dying to know what I think about everything?) all in one place: http://smarturl.it/PattiLarsenEmail.

Last—but not least!—I hope you enjoyed what you read! Your happiness is my happiness. And I'd love to hear just what you thought. A review where you found this book would mean the world to me—reviews feed writers more than you will ever know. So, loved it (or not so much), your honest review would make my day. Thank you!